MW01129224

One Step Back
A Titus Ray Thriller

the prequel to
One Night in Tehran

a novella by

LUANA EHRLICH

Visit the author's website LuanaEhrlich.com
or learn more about Titus Ray Thrillers here.

ISBN-10: 197592018X
ISBN-13: 9781975920180

To Ray Allan Pollock,
for giving an eleven-year-old girl
permission to read adult spy novels.

PART ONE

Chapter 1

Tehran, Iran
October 6, 2014

I was ahead of schedule. Even though I was supposed to meet my asset, Farid Kazim, near Zafaranieh Plaza at eleven o'clock, I was at the designated location an hour early.

Some Agency operatives might consider my early arrival a little excessive. They could be right.

On the other hand, those operatives hadn't been living in Tehran for the past two years.

I'd arrived in Iran two years ago as Hammid Salimi, the son of an Iranian watchmaker and a Swiss businesswoman. According to my legend—the false identity prepared for me by Support Services at the CIA—I was in Tehran to open up a market for my parents' line of luxury watches and jewelry.

In reality, I was in Tehran to identify potential assets who might be willing to help fund the opposition and topple the government.

To that end, I'd spent the last two years rubbing shoulders with some of the upper-class members of Iranian society, making friends with businessmen, as well as bankers, and cultivating ties with wealthy entrepreneurs.

During that time, I'd recruited six individuals who were now the core of my Iranian network. Three of them were bankers, two of them were businessmen, and one was a rich playboy.

Farid was the rich playboy.

His father, Asadi Kazim, owned three hotels in Iran; two in Tehran and one in Mashhad. All three of them had been built during the Shah's regime, and, when the Shah was ousted from power in 1979, Asadi had been allowed to keep the hotels.

According to Farid, his father had always been an ardent Islamist and had publically supported the revolution from the beginning. Allowing him to keep his hotels was the Supreme Leader's way of rewarding him.

Now, the Parisian Asadi Hotels were the only hotels in Iran with a five-star rating. However, the rooms were under constant surveillance by members of the Iranian Revolutionary Guard Corps (IRGC), and foreign dignitaries were warned to use caution when staying there.

Despite that, diplomats, as well as international investors, used the Asadi Hotels almost exclusively, and, in return, the IRGC supplemented Asadi Kazim's income for catering to them.

Outwardly, Farid appeared to be an Islamist like his father, but a few months after I'd recruited him, Farid had confessed to being an atheist.

I had my doubts about that.

While I believed Farid despised his father and blamed him for his mother's death, it was hard for me to believe a man who had been praying, fasting, and memorizing the Quran all his life didn't believe in a god of some sort.

Granted, I had no real belief system of my own, so I might not be the best person to judge someone else's faith.

Farid had chosen a passive aggressive method for exacting revenge on his father. His means of retribution included spending his father's fortune on expensive toys, associating with members of the Iranian opposition, and becoming a CIA asset.

As recruits go, Farid had been an easy target.

A member of one of the Iranian opposition groups, the People's Mojahedin Organization of Iran, had given me Farid's name, and I'd taken it from there.

After introducing myself to Farid at the wedding of a high-ranking IRGC official, I'd handed him my business card, and, in the midst of a discussion about the groom's father, I'd told Farid a less than flattering story about my father's treatment of my mother.

My anecdote was part of Hammid Salimi's fictional background and totally fabricated, but I could tell it resonated with him.

He'd called me a few days later.

Although he said he was calling because he wanted to purchase a watch for his girlfriend, when he showed up at my apartment, he seemed more interested in hearing about the hatred I had for my father than in buying my baubles and beads.

The two of us met often after that, and it wasn't long before I realized I'd become a kind of surrogate father to him. Since I was only in my late forties, I had a hard time identifying with this role, but it appeared to be working, so I went with it.

Within six months of meeting Farid, I'd recruited him as my asset. Now, not only was he feeding me intel from his contacts inside the IRGC, he was also supplying me with information about some of the guests at the Asadi hotels.

Douglas Carlton, the head of the Middle East desk at the CIA and my operations officer, had congratulated me on my recruitment of Farid during one of my rare video conferences with the Ops Center. I'd even seen him smile when I'd delivered Farid's first product—a recording of a conversation between a Russian general and a member of the Iranian President's security council.

Discerning how Carlton felt—even when I knew I'd exceeded his expectations—was never an easy task. On the other hand, he was sure to let me know exactly how he felt if I messed up—which I occasionally did.

With my own assets, I took the opposite approach. If the intel they delivered was an outstanding product, yielding measurable results, I showered them with praise—along with gifts or a bundle of cash. However, I seldom said anything about the superfluous stuff they dropped on me.

Today, I planned to commend Farid for the information he'd given me on the Syrian President's recent visit to Tehran. As a token of how useful Farid's information had been to the rebels trying to overthrow the Assad regime in Syria, I was planning to slip him an envelope full of American dollars.

When I glanced down at my watch, I realized I still had ten minutes left until Farid's scheduled arrival, and I decided there was enough time for me to do a third recon of the plaza.

Was I yielding to my compulsive tendencies by doing the extra recon?

Probably.

However, two years ago, when Carlton had briefed me on Operation Torchlight, he'd warned me about becoming complacent during my long-term assignment.

Although I didn't always listen to my boss, this time I did.

◆ ◆ ◆ ◆

Zafaranieh Plaza took up a full city block. It was bounded on one side by Ramkooh Boulevard and on the other side by Taheri Street. In the center of the block was a four-story shopping complex, and, along the outer perimeter, were a variety of restaurants and outdoor cafes.

The shopping center catered to the Versace and Pierre Cardin crowd, and an elaborate fountain at the entrance to the building was a testament to that. Reminiscent of the Latona Fountain in Versailles—minus the nude statues—it served as the focal point of Zafaranieh Plaza.

Surrounding the fountain were several stone benches, and I took a seat on one of them in order to keep an eye on the two men seated a few feet away.

Like most men in Tehran, they were dressed in long trousers, a collared shirt, and a sports jacket.

I wasn't particularly interested in their wearing apparel.

What caught my eye was their footwear.

It was the type of footwear worn by agents of VEVAK, the Iranian secret police; black leather half-boots with rubber soles and reinforced toes.

Both men were wearing a pair of the boots, and they were scuffed, well-worn, and in need of some black boot polish.

These men were obviously not new recruits.

As soon as I sat down, I spotted Farid making his way across the plaza. He was headed toward an outdoor café where he'd suggested we meet. Although he was staring down at his phone, I saw him look up occasionally and smile at a pretty girl.

One of the VEVAK agents, whose droopy black moustache reminded me of Joseph Stalin, glanced over at Farid.

After studying him for a few seconds, he looked away.

The younger agent, who was sitting next to him, gazed in my direction, sweeping his eyes over the crowd of people who were sitting around the fountain. Most of them were talking on their cell phones or gossiping with their friends.

Since I had no friends at Zafaranieh Plaza, I held my cell phone up to my ear and tried to ignore the VEVAK agent scrutinizing me.

I knew I didn't look that much different from the other males hanging around the plaza, despite the fact I was born in Flint, Michigan of Caucasian parents. Although my mother was of Polish descent, I'd inherited my father's coal black hair, brown eyes, and dark complexion.

When an Agency recruiter had interviewed me following my college graduation, he'd made several notations on the application in the section labeled, *"Applicant's Suitability for Covert Employment."*

Specifically, he'd placed checkmarks under various nationalities under the line item, *"The applicant has the physical characteristics necessary to blend in with the following ethnic groups."*

That was me, Titus Ray, the blender.

During my early days with the Agency, I'd been assigned to the Latin American desk, and I'd spent several years passing myself off as an Hispanic. Since being transferred to the Middle East desk, I'd been identified as a Syrian, an Iraqi, and a Jordanian. Now, while I was living in Tehran, I was an Iranian of mixed ancestry.

After spending a few minutes pretending to chat with someone, I put down my cell phone and glanced over at the VEVAK agent. He'd turned his attention elsewhere, so I strolled over to where Farid was seated at the outdoor café.

As soon as I greeted Farid, I saw Droopy Moustache get out of his seat and begin walking in my direction. The younger agent followed him a few seconds later.

◆ ◆ ◆ ◆

In spite of the fact I'd taught Farid some of the rudimentary elements of tradecraft, when I took a seat across from him, he continued texting on his cell phone, seemingly oblivious to the agents approaching our table.

I couldn't blame him.

I too felt invincible when I was his age.

As I observed the two VEVAK agents making their way across the plaza, I took out my Agency sat phone and entered a three-digit code, alerting the Ops Center I might be in VEVAK's crosshairs.

I knew the moment I'd entered the code, my location in Zafaranieh Plaza had instantaneously appeared on the CIA's Schematic Tracking Grid (STG), the hi-tech system used to monitor the movements of Agency operatives in the field during an operation.

Agency personnel called the system The Grid.

Now, my signal was showing up as a pulsating blue dot on The Grid's high-definition screen located in the basement of CIA headquarters in Langley, Virginia.

If I didn't cancel the code within fifteen minutes, a decision would have to be made. Carlton would be the one making that decision.

He'd have a couple of options at his disposal.

First, he could order the Agency's Reconnaissance and Signals Office (RSO) to reposition a satellite over Tehran. That would take some time, and, even though the images from a reconnaissance satellite were instructive for an ongoing crisis, they weren't that useful in determining what was happening in real time.

Carlton's other option would be to instruct the RSO to send a drone over Zafaranieh Plaza. Depending on the drone's location when Carlton issued the order, the Ops Center would be able to start receiving real time video from my position within fifteen minutes.

That option also had its drawbacks, because the Iranian military machine was very adept at detecting American drones who violated Iranian airspace, and, in the past, the Iranian generals had been quick to shoot them down.

Should that happen, sensational photographs of the disabled aircraft would be sent to every media outlet, and, within a matter of hours, those images would begin showing up on Jihadi networks around the globe. Eventually, those same images would be used in recruitment videos to target potential terrorists.

If I didn't cancel my distress code soon, Carlton had a third option.

He could choose to do nothing.

Then, everyone in the Ops Center would watch in silence as my pulsating dot went from blue to red and eventually disappeared off The Grid altogether.

Knowing Carlton, he would choose the third option.

After that, he would do everything in his power to negotiate my release from Evin Prison.

◆ ◆ ◆ ◆

A few seconds later, the two VEVAK agents brushed past Farid and me and headed inside the restaurant. Once they were out of sight, I picked up my Agency phone and entered the three-digit number cancelling the code.

I wanted to believe Carlton was relieved when he saw my pulsating dot go from blue to green.

I know I was.

"Hammid," Farid said, finally looking up from his phone, "I've been invited to attend General Suleiman's birthday party on Friday night. Are there any questions I should ask him?"

General Alizadeh Suleiman was a high-ranking member of the IRGC and the head of the Quds Force, a unit of the IRGC responsible for military operations overseas. Since taking over the Quds Force fifteen years ago, he'd reshaped the organization into a militant spy network with well-trained operatives capable of gathering intel from all around the world.

While the concept of Farid asking the general a few questions—questions of my own choosing—was appealing to me, the opportunity to do so seemed highly suspicious.

"I didn't know you were acquainted with the general, Farid."

Farid shrugged. "I don't really know him. He's one of my father's friends, but his birthday party is being held in the ballroom of the Parisian Asadi here in Tehran."

"If you don't know him, why did he send you an invitation to his party?"

Farid's eyes narrowed. "You're always so suspicious of everything, Hammid. It's just a birthday party. I get invited to lots of parties, especially if it's being held at one of my father's hotels."

The waiter appeared to take our order before I had a chance to respond, but then, when he walked away, I said, "I'm suspicious when something out of the ordinary happens."

"Well, in this case, if I didn't receive an invitation, you should be suspicious."

I nodded. "Okay, I get that, but you should still remain alert. And, Farid, please let me know if anyone shows you any extra attention."

He shook his head. "You can be assured no one pays any attention to me or anything I do. My mother was the only person who ever showed any interest in me and now she's dead."

Although I sometimes encouraged Farid to talk about his mother's death, instead of feeding his self-pity issues today, I tried to instill some confidence in him.

"You're right, Farid. the general's party sounds like the ideal time to ask him a few questions. I'll get back to you before Friday and let you know what to ask him."

He smiled. "Should I see if I could get you an invitation to the party?"

"I appreciate the offer, but that's probably not a good idea. General Suleiman is no fool. It might look suspicious to him if a watch salesman showed up at his birthday celebration and began asking him questions. You'll do a much better job."

Farid seemed pleased with my response. Then, when I gave him an envelope full of cash for the excellent intel he'd delivered on

President Assad's visit to Tehran, he looked even more pleased.

As he slipped the envelope inside his jacket pocket, a man suddenly appeared at our table. The moment I realized who he was, I felt certain the focus of Operation Torchlight was about to change.

I wasn't wrong about that.

Chapter 2

Farid didn't appear nervous when he glanced up and saw the man standing there. Instead, as was customary in the Middle East when two male acquaintances greeted each other, he got up and kissed him on both cheeks.

As they embraced, Farid said, "*As-salamu 'alaykum.*"

The man returned Farid's greeting of peace. "*W 'alaykumu s-salam.*"

Farid gestured at me. "Hammid, allow me to introduce you to my friend, Amir."

After we shook hands, Farid invited Amir to join us. When he sat down, Farid gave him a brief description of who I was—the son of Talib Salimi, the famous Iranian watchmaker. In turn, Farid sketched out a brief bio of Amir for me.

I listened politely, but I already knew who his friend was.

He was Amir Madani, one of Iran's nuclear scientists. I'd recognized him as soon as he'd greeted Farid.

Although Operation Torchlight didn't include the protocols for making contact with anyone in Iran's nuclear community, I was excited about the possibility of getting to know Amir Madani.

My excitement was motivated by the incompetency of the CIA's Nuclear Security Division (NSD), the department responsible for providing intelligence on countries capable of producing nuclear weapons.

The NSD had an abysmal track record in Iran.

For years, the NSD's administrators had defended their failure by insisting it was impossible to make contact with any of Iran's nuclear scientists, primarily because the Iranian regime maintained an extremely tight rein on these individuals.

However, Mossad, the Israeli intelligence agency, had been sharing intel with the CIA on Iran's nuclear program for several years now. More often than not, they had identified those secrets as having come from scientists in Iran who were eager to hand over information on Iran's nuclear weapons program.

According to Carlton, this glaring discrepancy in the intelligence-gathering capabilities of the two agencies was fast becoming an embarrassment to the suits on the seventh floor.

The best intel the CIA had ever been able to obtain on Iran's nuclear program had come from the recruitment of Komeil Haddadi, one of Iran's premier nuclear scientists.

However, his recruitment hadn't been the result of any effort on the part of the CIA.

Five years ago, Komeil Haddadi had eluded his security handlers at a World Nuclear Association Conference in London and made his way over to the American Embassy, where he'd surprised everyone by asking for asylum.

Even though no one had seen that coming, Carlton, along with several other Agency personnel, had been on a flight to London within twenty-four hours to begin debriefing him.

When I was introduced to Komeil a few years after his defection, he was quick to let me know he'd been planning his escape from Iran for years.

As part of my preparation for Operation Torchlight, Support Services had arranged for me to meet regularly with Komeil at his home near Washington, D.C. I'd requested the meetings because I wanted to familiarize myself with the peculiarities of the Iranian culture and to perfect my fluency in Farsi, the language spoken in Iran.

Since I'd never had any formal training in Farsi—having only picked up the basics from an Iranian exile living across the hall from me during my stint in Pakistan—Komeil had spent several hours a day schooling me in the finer points of Farsi grammar.

During our time together, he'd also briefed me on some of the more prominent people in Tehran, people he thought might be sympathetic to an overthrow of the Iranian regime. Most of these individuals were bankers and lawyers, but some of his scientific buddies had also been included.

To make it easier for me to identify these people, we'd spent hours sifting through stacks of photographs prepared for us by the Agency's counterintelligence analysts.

One day, near the end of our time together, Komeil had shown me a photograph of some of his colleagues. It was a group shot taken at a conference on nuclear physics. Among those attendees was Amir Madani.

Now, the man himself was sitting across from me.

◆ ◆ ◆ ◆

I was eager to learn how Farid and Amir Madani had met, but when Farid referenced a series of lectures Amir had delivered during a symposium at Tehran University, I realized they must have met at the university.

Farid's mention of the symposium seemed like the perfect opening for me to show some interest in Amir. I asked him, "What was the subject matter of the symposium?"

"It focused on the role of science and technology in government. My lectures primarily addressed the responsibility scientists have to use their research for the betterment of society."

Farid had never shown any interest in either science or the betterment of society, so I was mystified as to why he had attended Amir's lectures in the first place. However, a few minutes later, when Amir brought up Farid's girlfriend, I realized she must have persuaded him to attend the lectures.

"I enjoyed talking with Chaman at the symposium," Amir told Farid. "Your girlfriend asked me some very thought-provoking questions."

Farid's latest girlfriend, Chaman Bijan, was the daughter of a wealthy telecomm executive, but, like Farid, she had a bit of a rebellious streak in her. In fact, a few weeks ago, when Farid had introduced us, Chaman had told me she preferred to think of herself as an activist, although she wasn't specific about the causes she supported.

Farid said, "I hope you didn't think Chaman was being disrespectful when we attended your lecture, Amir. She never passes up an opportunity to challenge the status quo."

Amir assured Farid he hadn't been offended by Chaman's questions, and, as if to prove his sincerity, he asked Farid some questions about her.

Soon, those questions turned into more questions, and before long, Amir appeared to be interrogating Farid instead of having a conversation with him.

Farid didn't seem the least bit concerned he was giving Amir a lot of information about Chaman; instead, Farid appeared flattered by Amir's interest in his girlfriend.

By the time I was able to steer the conversation on to a different topic, I felt certain Amir knew what restaurants Chaman frequented, where she shopped for her clothes, and even the name of the apartment building where she lived.

While I found Amir's questioning of Farid unusual, I attributed his information-gathering technique to his scientific mindset, and I dismissed any thought he could be a threat to Farid.

A few minutes later, Amir asked me a question.

"Tell me, Hammid; are you originally from Iran?"

To prove my theory about Amir's inquisitive nature, I proceeded to give him a few short answers about my background to see if my answers piqued his curiosity.

"No, I was born in Geneva, Switzerland."

He raised his eyebrows. "Really?"

"Yes, my mother is a Swiss national."

"But your father's an Iranian, right?"

I nodded. "That's right."

"Did they meet in Iran?"

Since the pace of Amir's questions had picked up, I decided it was time to flesh out my answers a little more. By adding a few details, I was hoping to make a connection with Amir that would eventually lead to a friendship. If I became friends with one of Iran's nuclear scientist, the payoff could be enormous, especially if I managed to recruit him as my asset.

Of course, that was a big if.

"No," I said, "my parents didn't meet here in Iran. They met at a jewelry exposition in Geneva. My father was at the expo looking for new markets for his watchmaking, and my mother was at the expo representing her father's jewelry business."

Amir gave a short laugh. "Which came first? The business relationship or the personal one?"

I felt certain Amir's lighthearted question was a good sign our conversation was headed in the right direction, so I smiled and said, "My mother insists it was purely business at first, but my father claims it was a little of both."

Amir nodded. "Everything depends on perspective, right?"

At this point, I fully expected Amir to ask me some follow-up questions about growing up in Switzerland or, at the very least, quiz me about what I was doing in Iran. Instead, he glanced down at his watch.

"I really need to get back to work now. I didn't realize it was getting so late."

"Perhaps you need a new watch," I said, handing him my business card. "Whenever it's convenient, I'd be happy to drop by your office and show you our new line of timepieces."

He chuckled when he took my card. "It was nice meeting you, Hammid, but I don't believe I could afford a Salimi watch."

As I watched Amir Madani walk away from the table, I wondered if I'd been wrong about him. Had I been too quick to attribute his interrogation of Farid to his scientific mindset or was his real motivation his desire to learn more about Chaman?

Whatever his motivation was, I couldn't deny the nuclear scientist had just spent the last thirty minutes gathering intel on Chaman Bijan.

Now, I was determined to find out why.

◆ ◆ ◆ ◆

As Farid and I watched Amir making his way across Zafaranieh Plaza, I was tempted to lecture my asset about the need to be more judicious in his conversations with people, but then I decided that wasn't such a good idea.

Farid's friends and acquaintances saw him as an easygoing, free-wheeling kind of guy, and if I tried to stifle his exuberant nature, his contacts might become suspicious of him or stop communicating with him altogether.

I wanted Farid to be seen as a rich, harmless playboy because people shared secrets with rich, harmless playboys.

I gestured at Amir's retreating figure. "He's an interesting guy."

Farid shook his head. "He may be interesting, but I could barely stay awake during his lectures."

"How did Chaman feel about his lectures?"

"She found them fascinating, but she was disappointed in their content. She said she expected Amir to offer a few more progressive ideas about Iran's place in the world."

"What does Chaman consider progressive?"

He shrugged. "With Chaman, it's hard to tell."

I prodded him. "Did she object to the way Amir presented Iran's nuclear program?"

"No, she didn't care about that. What bothered her was Amir's failure to address the issue of how dependent we are on Russia for research in the nuclear energy field. She said she knew he felt strongly about our scientists conducting their own research, and he wasn't happy about Iran relying on Russia for that data."

"I'm guessing she made her views known to Amir."

He nodded. "They discussed it during the question and answer period. She didn't back down when he told her he was rethinking his position on Russia."

"Why was Chaman so certain they were on the same page when it came to nuclear energy?"

"Her father serves on the AEOI Board of Directors with Amir, and he told her it was something he and Amir had often discussed."

Several years ago, Iran's Supreme Leader had established the Atomic Energy Organization of Iran (AEOI). Its purpose was to develop applications for the use of nuclear technology in commercial ventures, but I was surprised to hear Amir was a member of their board. According to Komeil, the AEOI Board was made up of wealthy businessmen, not underpaid nuclear scientists.

"Are you sure Amir's on the AEOI Board?"

"I'm positive. According to Chaman, Amir is heavily invested in a nuclear power plant south of the city. I'm sure that's why they asked him to be a member of their board."

I couldn't hide my surprise at this revelation, and Farid immediately commented on it. "You look surprised, Hammid. I thought you knew about the power plant."

I nodded. "I knew about the power plant, but I was surprised to hear a government-paid scientist could afford to invest in it."

"I don't believe Amir's salary could be the source of his investment funds."

"What then?"

"I'm guessing his money comes from an inheritance."

"So if Amir has capital to invest, why did he say he couldn't afford a Salimi watch?"

"Amir had to be kidding about that. He has plenty of money."

"You're sure about that?"

Farid nodded. "During his lecture, he mentioned he lived in Shemiran, and I know apartments there don't come cheap."

I knew all about Shemiran. It was a luxury apartment complex north of Tehran. Before I left Langley, when I was being briefed by Support Services about where Hammid Salimi would be living in Tehran, I'd suggested buying him an apartment in Shemiran.

Robert Ira, the Agency's Deputy Director of Operations, had immediately nixed the idea. He said the cost of purchasing an apartment there would put Operation Torchlight over budget, and he didn't believe my presence there would yield enough intel to offset the extra expenditure.

Now, I wondered if the DDO might change his mind about that, especially if he knew setting me up in an apartment in Shemiran would put me in close proximity to one of Iran's nuclear scientists.

Before making such a proposal, though, I needed to know more about Amir Madani, particularly why he'd shown so much interest in Chaman Bijan.

Right now, I was betting his interest in her was purely personal.

I understood that.

Chaman was a beautiful woman, extremely intelligent, and not shy about expressing her feelings—a combination most men found irresistible.

I know I did.

However, that wasn't the reason I decided to pay Chaman a visit. I did it for operational purposes only.

Really.

Chapter 3

Chaman lived in an apartment building on Maryam Street, in the affluent Elahyieh district of northern Tehran, not far from the Russian Embassy. Her building, Shahre Tower, was one of several high-rises in the area.

One of the assets I was running, a banker named Omid Askari, lived in a three-story house about a mile from Chaman's apartment. I'd been inside his luxurious residence once, but no one was home at the time.

The sign outside Shahre Tower indicated there was parking available in an underground garage; however, I opted to park my black BMW directly across the street from Chaman's building.

After squeezing my vehicle between a Peugeot and a Mercedes, I pulled a pair of binoculars out of the glove compartment and did a quick recon of the area just to make sure no one living at Shahre Tower had drawn the attention of VEVAK.

Along with several apartment buildings, Maryam Street was home to a couple of high-end boutiques, an art gallery, and a restaurant with patio seating.

While no one on the busy street particularly drew my attention, a man and woman seated at one of the restaurant's outdoor tables momentarily sparked my interest, especially after I noticed the man was occasionally glancing over at the entrance to Shahre Tower.

After watching him for several minutes, I realized his eyes were only drifting in the direction of Chaman's apartment building when the woman seated across from him wasn't speaking to him. I finally decided his sporadic activity was an innocent reaction to the conversation they were having.

From what I could tell, he was looking away from the woman before he responded to her, as if he needed to compose his thoughts by staring off in the distance for a moment or two.

As a processor, I understood what he was doing—he was buying himself a little extra time to consider things and to anticipate how the woman might react to what he was going to say to her.

After a few minutes, I put away the field glasses and exited my vehicle.

By the time I'd entered the lobby of Shahre Tower, I'd already scripted out what I was going to say to Chaman when she answered her doorbell. I knew I couldn't use the I-was-just-in-the-neighborhood excuse to explain why I was paying her a visit, because Chaman knew I lived in an apartment near the Kharazi Expressway in western Tehran.

Instead, I'd decided to go for the straightforward approach.

◆ ◆ ◆ ◆

There was no mistaking the surprised look on Chaman's face when she opened the door to her penthouse apartment and saw me standing there.

"I'm sorry, Chaman," I said. "I know I should have called before I showed up on your doorstep."

"Do you even have my number?" she asked, motioning me inside.

"No, I don't believe I do. Would you mind giving it to me?"

She tilted her pretty head slightly to the right and smiled at me. "And why would I do that, Hammid?"

"Oh, I don't know," I said, returning her smile. "What if Farid had an emergency when we were out together, and I needed to call you?"

She didn't respond until we'd entered her living room. It was a room filled with expensive furnishings and decorated in pale ivory and shimmering gold, a color combination I'd often seen used in the homes of other wealthy Iranians.

After pointing me toward an ornate sofa, she sat down in a high-back chair opposite me. As she positioned her legs modestly in front of her, she said, "You're right, Hammid. You should have my phone number."

I waited a beat or two, expecting her to recite the number for me, but then, when she didn't, I said, "You're probably wondering why I dropped in on you like this."

"It does seem a little out of character for you."

Since we barely knew each other, I wasn't sure why she thought I wasn't the spontaneous type, but I agreed with her assessment anyway. "You're right. I like to plan things out well in advance, but a matter has come up unexpectedly, and I couldn't wait to discuss it with you."

She leaned forward in her chair. "What is it?"

"I'm sure Farid told you I'm seeking investors for my parents' jewelry business."

She nodded. "Farid tells me everything."

I knew that wasn't true, but correcting her wasn't in my best interest, so I let it go.

"I'm only interested in investors who are committed to our product, and who are well positioned to make a long-term investment. When I—"

"Is that why you're here, Hammid?" she asked, leaning back in her chair. "Do you want my father to invest in your—"

"No, Chaman, of course not," I said, interrupting her. "I'm here to ask your opinion about someone. I've seen how Farid values your judgment, especially about people, and I'd like to get your take on someone who has expressed an interest in becoming an investor in Salimi watches."

A smile returned to her face. "I've been told I have a gift for reading people."

"I don't doubt that."

She pushed a strand of hair away from her eyes. "Okay, so tell me about your investor."

"He's a government scientist named Amir Madani. Farid introduced us, and I understand he's also one of your father's acquaintances."

She nodded. "That's right."

"I'm guessing you know him as well."

Her eyes narrowed. "Yes, I know Amir, but if I owned Salami watches, I wouldn't allow him to invest in my company."

"Really?" I said, trying to look surprised. "Why is that?"

"Because Amir Madani isn't the man he appears to be."

◆ ◆ ◆ ◆

After commending Chaman for her honesty, I encouraged her to tell me what she knew about Amir. As it turned out, she knew very little, but that didn't stop her from making some derogatory comments about him.

"He's completely disingenuous," she said. "One day, he told my father he was against Russia's involvement in our country, but a week later, when he had an opportunity to speak at Tehran University on the subject, he said something completely different."

"Perhaps he had simply changed his mind about the Russians."

"Well, that's what he said, but if you believe strongly in something, you don't change your mind that easily."

Chaman was typical of other young people I'd met in Iran who were born into wealthy families. Even though they lived in Iran's repressed society, most of them didn't think twice about expressing their opinion on controversial subjects. I suspected they weren't afraid of speaking out because they knew their privileged position would shield them from being punished by the regime.

On the other hand, the less fortunate Iranians—those poor souls who couldn't afford to bribe someone should they be arrested for making contentious comments—seldom voiced their opinions, especially in public.

"So you and Amir discussed his change of attitude?"

She nodded. "After the seminar, I asked him why he'd chosen to lie about his beliefs."

"Was this a private conversation?"

For a brief moment, I thought Chaman looked uncomfortable. "No,

I confronted him during the public question-and-answer period following his lecture."

"I see."

"Look, Hammid," she said, pointing her manicured finger at me, "I realize some people might think that was rude of me, but I'm an activist; that's what I do."

"I'm not sure I understand what you mean by that, Chaman. What do you do as an activist?"

She got out of her chair and walked over to a set of windows facing Maryam Street. "I confront people, especially if they're not being true to their beliefs. I call attention to injustices, no matter what they are."

She turned around and motioned for me to join her. "Come here, Hammid. I'll show you what I mean."

Even though I knew Chaman considered herself a "modern" Iranian woman and didn't necessarily adhere to the strict Islamic teachings forbidding physical contact between an unmarried man and woman, I was careful not to stand too close to her when I walked over to the window, lest I accidently brush up against her.

She pointed down at the street. "See that art gallery down there? The one on the corner by the restaurant?"

"Yes, I noticed it when I was entering your building."

She turned away from the window and faced me. "When the gallery owners refused to display the works of the Saudi artist, Raja Abu, I had my father notify them he wouldn't renew their lease if they weren't willing to display his paintings."

"I'm sure that got their attention."

She nodded. "Exactly. That's what I mean by being an activist. Many of Abu's paintings are controversial because he depicts injustices in Islamic society, but I thought it was unfair for the gallery owners to censor him here in Tehran if art galleries in Riyadh were willing to exhibit his works."

"Perhaps the gallery owners were simply being cautious about featuring the Saudi artist because of the animosity between Riyadh and Tehran. Maybe it had nothing to do with the paintings themselves."

Chaman looked puzzled. "I'm not sure I know what you mean. Iran has always maintained close relations with all of our Arab neighbors, despite our differences."

I suddenly realized Chaman probably didn't know about the tense standoff between Tehran and Riyadh regarding Iran's role in the Syrian conflict; such information wasn't usually broadcast on the evening news in Tehran.

I said, "I'm referring to the conflict between the Sunni and Shiite sects of Islam. Perhaps the gallery owners didn't want to display the works of a Sunni artist when the majority of Iranians are Shia."

Chaman laughed. "But don't you see, Hammid? That too is an injustice. It's the same thing I told Amir Madani. Don't be afraid to go against the majority, especially if you feel strongly about something."

"Did Amir agree with you?"

"No, I don't believe he did. Or, if he did, he wasn't willing to admit it." She shook her head. "That's what I mean. Amir Madani is too indecisive to be a good investor for your company."

"I'm afraid you're right, Chaman."

I immediately turned away from the window and headed toward the door. "I should go inform Amir of my decision right away. Do you know where he works?"

She seemed startled by my sudden departure. "Ah . . . I believe he works at the Energy Building across from the Defense Ministry, but you know you won't be able to get in there without a security pass."

"You're right. I'll need to call Amir first and make an appointment to meet him somewhere."

Chaman followed me to the front door. When I reached the foyer, I placed my hand over my heart in an effort to display my sincerity.

"I'm grateful for your help, Chaman. Thank you."

"You're welcome, Hammid."

When I turned to leave, I felt her fingers brush lightly across my back. "You can call me anytime, Hammid. 021-77424832."

I was smiling as I walked away.

Chapter 4

After my conversation with Chaman, I had mixed feelings about pursuing a friendship with Amir as a means of recruiting him as my asset.

Although Chaman had verified Amir's willingness to criticize the Iranian regime—at least on the question of its partnership with Russia—I questioned whether this was enough evidence to indicate the scientist would be a viable CIA asset.

Perhaps, like Chaman, Amir wasn't afraid to denounce certain government practices because he knew his wealth and position would protect him from any kind of hostile response from the Iranian regime.

However, such outspokenness didn't necessarily mean he would be open to an approach from a foreign entity.

I also had my doubts about whether I could persuade him to betray his country by offering him large sums of cash. Apparently, Amir Madani was already a man of means.

Amir's wealth was a big concern to me—not the money itself, but where it came from.

I wanted to know the source of his funds.

Had he inherited his riches as Farid had suggested?

Perhaps.

But there were several other possibilities, and some of them could be hazardous to my health, not to mention my life.

The most dangerous possibility was that Amir was on the payroll of VEVAK.

If the secret police were paying him to spy on his fellow scientists—not an unusual practice in an authoritarian society—then, more than likely, he had been trained in basic espionage techniques.

Such techniques included how to assess threat risks and spot suspicious behavior, which meant Amir might view someone who showed an interest in him a little differently than most people would.

In that event, he might request VEVAK's assistance in assessing my intentions, and while my legend could easily pass a superficial inspection, it might not hold up if VEVAK ordered a deep data dig into my background.

Another possibility was that Amir was already on the payroll of a foreign government.

The Israelis immediately came to mind.

The North Koreans were another option, given their recent history with other nuclear scientists. However, since Mossad, the Israeli intelligence agency, usually paid their informants in large sums of cash, the Israelis appeared to be the most likely candidate for recruiting Amir.

While Mossad and the CIA played on the same team when it came to sharing intelligence with each other, when it came to recruiting assets, it was a different story.

In that narrative, the two agencies often engaged in a fierce battle to win what had always been considered the highest prize in counterintelligence—a highly placed government source.

At times, the competition between the two agencies had even gotten ugly.

For years, I'd heard rumors Mossad had once blown a CIA operation wide open just to prevent one of their own Syrian assets from being recruited. While I doubted the story's veracity in its entirety, if it turned out Amir was working for the Israelis, I would stay as far away from him as possible.

My reluctance to mix it up with Mossad wasn't based on my fear of what they could do to me.

It was based on a promise I'd made several years ago when one of their operatives had helped me out of a tough spot in Lebanon. After that, I'd vowed to be as supportive of my Israeli counterparts as possible.

As long as it didn't jeopardize America's interests, I planned to keep that promise.

◆ ◆ ◆ ◆

After spending several hours weighing all my options, I realized I couldn't pass up the opportunity to make a run at Amir.

The Iranian nuclear scientist was just too big a prize.

Eventually, I'd have to contact Carlton and get him to sign off on reworking the protocols of Operation Torchlight to include pursuing Amir Madani as my asset. But, before I did that, I needed to spend a few days running surveillance on him.

That would be the first question Carlton would ask me if I sent him an emergency contact request. My operations officer considered running surveillance on a potential target as doing one's homework, and not doing one's homework was seen as incompetence.

Carlton had a thing about incompetence—he didn't tolerate it.

Having learned from Chaman where Amir worked—at the Atomic Energy Building—and from Farid where Amir lived—in Shemiran—I immediately scouted out both neighborhoods.

Of the two sites, the neighborhood around Shemiran proved to be the most desirable location for setting up surveillance on him. Parking was permitted on the street opposite his building, plus, within walking distance, there were several restaurants, a couple of coffee shops, and a grocery store.

I was betting Amir frequented at least one of those establishments, and since they were all public places, if he was employed by VEVAK, then they would also be the most likely spots for him to meet up with a VEVAK agent, or hand off information to a courier without drawing anyone's attention.

Such contact was sometimes difficult to detect without using a team of watchers, but, unfortunately, I had no such resources in Tehran.

My assignment was strictly deep cover. I had no partner, no

embassy backup, no surveillance teams. Unlike other missions where I usually operated out of the American embassy or from a fully-staffed safe house, I was on my own in Iran.

Operating solo had never bothered me that much.

In fact, I actually preferred it. But, in this case, I wouldn't have minded having a couple of Agency surveillance teams with me. That way, I would have been able to keep tabs on Amir 24/7.

Since that wasn't possible, I did an economized version of a full surveillance package.

◆ ◆ ◆ ◆

The day after I visited with Chaman, I arrived at Shemiran early enough in the afternoon to find a parking spot on the street outside the apartment complex.

If nothing else, on my first day, I wanted to at least identify the kind of car he was driving when he returned home from work.

Just before dusk, I saw Amir pull into the parking lot on the west side of the complex. The lot offered covered carports as well as enclosed garages, and, after making a call to the main office, I'd found out the garages were reserved for those fortunate tenants who own one of Shemiran's higher-end apartments.

It didn't surprise me when I saw Amir drive his black Mercedes S-Class sedan into one of the garages. A few seconds later, he walked out of the unit and entered a code on the security panel on the outside wall. Once he saw the door descend, he walked around to the main entrance of Building B and went inside.

For the next week, I followed Amir everywhere he went. He usually left Building B around eight o'clock in the morning and arrived at the Defense Ministry's military compound around nine o'clock. It wasn't unusual for him to take a two-hour lunch, but since several of his co-workers usually accompanied him to one of the nearby restaurants, I saw no opportunity for him to meet up with anyone who might be running him as an agent.

One afternoon, I got a break as I was sitting in my car outside the military installation waiting for Amir to leave work for the day.

I happened to notice one of his colleagues, a young guy who often joined him for lunch, had a flat tire on the left rear wheel of his older model Fiat.

He'd just driven out of the main security gate, and I knew the guy couldn't get very far down the road without having to pull over, so I decided to follow him and play the role of a Good Samaritan.

Even though I had to abandon my surveillance of Amir, I knew if I was able to pick up some new intel about the scientist, it would be worth it.

As expected, I spotted the Fiat on the side of the road about a mile down the highway.

I pulled in directly behind him.

"Hey," I said to the Flat Tire Guy as we both got out of our vehicles, "I've been trying to get your attention. I was right behind you when you pulled out the front gate, and I couldn't believe the security guy didn't let you know you had a flat tire."

He shook his head as he looked down at the tire. "You know Farshid, he's an idiot."

I added an appropriate disparaging comment about Farshid, and then I offered to help him remove the damaged tire.

"Sure," he said. "I could use your help."

He extended his hand toward me. "I'm Merza Zand."

"Yousef Navid," I said. "I work in the Defense Ministry. Actually, I'm in Procurements."

Merza nodded. "I work over at the Energy Building next door." He gestured toward my BMW. "With a car like that, I knew you had to work in Defense. Research scientists get paid next to nothing."

I tried to look embarrassed. "My father got me the job."

After we removed the flat tire, I said. "You work in atomic research, huh? You must be one smart guy."

He smiled. "I don't work alone. There are several other guys on my team."

"It still sounds like interesting work."

"Yeah, it's pretty interesting." When he glanced up at me, he gave me a wary look. "You know I can't talk about it, right?"

"Oh, absolutely," I said with a smile. "I'm not even sure I'd want to know what goes on in the Energy Building."

He nodded. "Believe me. You don't."

Having learned Amir Madani wasn't just any nuclear scientist, but a nuclear scientist involved in atomic research, I executed a short fist pump once I got back in my car and headed toward Shemiran.

Now, it was time to call Carlton.

Chapter 5

Tehran, Iran
October 14, 2014

Contacting my operations officer was easy. All I had to do was enter a three-digit code on my Agency sat phone.

How soon Carlton got back with me would depend on the three numbers I decided to enter on the keypad. One set of numbers would let Carlton know I needed to speak with an entire operations team in one of the Real Time Management (RTM) Centers located in the basement of CIA headquarters at Langley.

The RTM Centers were collectively known as the Ops Center, which was where the day-to-day operations of the CIA took place.

If I entered that code, I might not hear back from Carlton for an hour, maybe even two hours, depending on how long it took him to assemble the RTM team running Operation Torchlight.

On the other hand, if I chose to punch in a different set of numbers, then Carlton would know I only wanted a one-on-one conversation with him. In that case, I'd probably get a call within fifteen minutes.

Since my operations officer always preferred to be told about a matter before calling in the entire operations team, I entered the code alerting Carlton I wanted to have a chat with him without an operations team present.

If Carlton followed his usual pattern when I gave him fresh intel, once I told him about Amir, he would ask my opinion about setting up a video call with the entire operations team to discuss the protocols for handling the new material.

Then, if I followed my usual pattern, after pretending to think about it a second, I'd tell him that decision was entirely up to him.

Carlton would never admit it, but he enjoyed making decisions, and I tried to indulge him as much as possible.

◆ ◆ ◆ ◆

Although my Agency satellite phone was a fully encrypted model, with added safeguards to prevent anyone listening in on my conversations or being able to capture my text messages, I took one extra precaution after sending Carlton the contact code.

Next to the armchair in my living room, I placed what appeared to be an alarm clock. In reality, it was a sound distortion device or Acoustical Protection System (APS), which rendered all voices in the room as static and thwarted any listening devices in the area.

Eleven minutes after I keyed in the three-digit code, my phone vibrated.

"Is this official?" Carlton asked.

"That depends."

According to Agency regulations, when an intelligence officer contacted his operations officer, that contact had to be recorded for the official log. Although Carlton wasn't a rule-breaker, he sometimes defined the wording in Agency documents a little differently than the CIA's Legal Division did.

For example, Carlton didn't believe it was necessary to record every single conversation, just those conversations labeled official. However, I always left it up to him to define what he meant by official.

"Depends on what?" he asked.

"On whether or not you want it on the official record that I recently made contact with one of Iran's nuclear scientists."

"Does this have anything to do with the 319 you sent the Ops Center a week ago?"

The signal I'd sent the Ops Center when I'd noticed the two

VEVAK agents approaching our table in Zafaranieh Plaza was called the Emergency Locator and Monitoring Alert. However, it was usually referred to as a 319, the numbers I'd entered on the keypad.

"No, that was a false alarm, although that *was* the day I met the nuclear scientist in question."

"Am I correct in assuming this call is simply to report the initial contact with that individual?"

"I guess you could put it that way."

"Well, I *am* putting it that way, and, since that's the case, I see no reason to make an official recording of this conversation."

"Works for me."

"So tell me about this nuclear scientist."

I gave Carlton a detailed accounting of everything I knew about Amir Madani, beginning with my first encounter with him in Zafaranieh Plaza and ending with the conversation I'd had with Merza Zand about the type of work he and Madani were doing in the Atomic Energy Building.

Carlton was a big note taker, and, every now and then, I could hear him flipping pages on his yellow notepad.

I knew his notepad was yellow, because, for as long as I'd known him, I'd never seen him taking notes on anything other than a yellow legal pad. Later, he would transfer his notes to a computer, and then he'd methodically tear off each yellow sheet from his notepad and feed them through his paper shredder.

He would do this individual sheet by individual sheet.

When I'd finished briefing him on Amir, he said, "It's good to hear you've done your homework, Titus, but what's your end game here? Do you really believe you have a chance of recruiting Amir Madani?"

Although I could hear the skepticism in his voice, I also detected a note of excitement, and I knew he had to be considering what recruiting Madani would mean for the Agency as well as for his own career.

"Admit it, Douglas. He's an enticing prospect."

"Enticing or not, his finances are a red flag. We'll need to take a hard look at them."

♦ ♦ ♦ ♦

Even though Carlton refused to admit the prospect of having one of Iran's nuclear research scientist on the payroll of the CIA would be a major coup for the Agency, he immediately began outlining the steps he would take to ensure Amir Madani wasn't already on the radar of another intelligence agency or possibly on the payroll of VEVAK.

"I'll contact Katherine and have her check him out," he said. "She owes me a few favors, so I'm sure she'll expedite my request."

Katherine Broward was the Agency's chief strategic analyst. Her department, the Analysis and Strategic Assessment (ASA) division, was responsible for assembling, processing, and evaluating all the information and data collected from intelligence sources. The ASA desk also had the means to hack into banks, businesses, and foreign governments, as well as open sources, such as the internet and media outlets.

"In the meantime," Carlton said, "continue your surveillance on Madani."

"Of course."

"Katherine should be able to get back to me in a couple of days, but don't approach Madani until I see what our analysts have turned up on him."

"Would you also have Support Services find out if there's an apartment available in Shemiran?"

"Why would I do that?"

"Because I'm convinced the easiest way for me to cultivate a friendship with Amir is to have an apartment in Shemiran. By living in the same apartment complex, I'll have plenty of opportunities to run into him, and since I'm running solo here, it will be the best means I have for keeping tabs on his activities."

Carlton didn't say anything for a few seconds.

Finally, he said, "Are you forgetting the DDO vetoed the idea of purchasing an apartment for you in Shemiran? If I remember correctly, he said the cost was prohibitive."

"He might change his mind when he learns that buying an apartment in Shemiran would give me 24/7 access to an Iranian nuclear scientist."

Carlton sighed. "I'll have Support Services see if there's anything available. Any other questions?"

I tried to phrase my next question carefully, because I knew Carlton was adamant about not commenting on rumors floating around Langley. At the same time, I also knew he took great delight in imparting information no one else knew.

His willingness to answer my next question would depend on how precisely I was able to draw the distinction between the two.

I said, "I'm sure the DDO is the only person who has this information, Douglas, but is it possible my efforts to pursue Amir as my asset would compromise another ongoing operation in Iran?"

"Are you referring to the NSD?"

Geographically, the Nuclear Security Division's territory overlapped all divisions within the Agency. In order to prevent the possibility of two different divisions running operations targeting the same asset, the DDO was responsible for informing the division heads of any ongoing operations.

"Yes," I said, "I'm talking about the NSD. I wouldn't want to be playing around in their backyard over here."

"Are you kidding me? The NSD hasn't obtained a single piece of actionable intel in Iran since they learned the Ayatollah was trying to procure illicit nuclear material."

I lied and said, "I didn't realize that."

My comment triggered a long response from Carlton regarding how much he knew about how the NSD had tried—and subsequently failed—to recruit Iran's nuclear scientists.

When he'd finished outlining the division's incompetency, he assured me the DDO would inform the NSD if he gave me the go ahead to pursue Amir.

He added, "As far as I know, the NSD doesn't have any ongoing operations that would interfere with you running Amir as your asset. We'll know more once we get Katherine's report."

After he commented on the intel Farid had been able to obtain on General Suleiman, he returned to the subject of Amir Madani.

"If Katherine's data mining doesn't turn up anything on Madani, what's your opinion about having the DDO assemble an operations team so we can put together some protocols on how you should handle Madani?"

"That's your call, Douglas. I'll leave it up to you to make that decision."

◆ ◆ ◆ ◆

Two days after my initial call to Carlton about Amir Madani, I received a flash alert from the Ops Center. It was in the form of a text message in Farsi from a local dry-cleaning establishment.

"Your laundry is ready for pickup," it said.

When I received the text, I was parked outside Amir's apartment building, but I immediately abandoned my post and headed back to my apartment on the other side of Tehran.

There was heavy traffic on the Kharazi Expressway, and by the time I arrived at my apartment, almost an hour had passed since I'd received the alert.

It took me another twenty minutes to get my laptop set up, attach the encryption devices, and turn on the APS equipment. Despite the delay, when Carlton's image pixilated across my screen, I thought he looked pleased.

"Your timing's perfect," he said, glancing down at his watch. "I've asked Katherine to join us, and she's just texted me she's on her way up to my office."

Carlton was using the small conference room next door to his office, which he usually did when he presented his operatives with a data readout or updated them on an operation's change in status.

While his choice of venue indicated he wasn't ready to call in a full operations team yet, the fact that he'd asked Katherine to brief me in person about what her analysts had turned up on Amir Madani made me think the status of Operation Torchlight was about to change.

As I was updating Carlton on my continuing surveillance of Madani, the door to the conference room swung open and Carlton's executive assistant, Sally Jo Hartford, escorted Katherine inside.

Carlton, who was seated at the head of the rectangular table, immediately got to his feet when the two women entered the room.

Once Sally Jo had left, he gestured at the chair on his left and said, "Katherine, please be seated."

As soon as she sat down, she glanced up at the screen and smiled at me.

"Titus, I don't think I've seen you with a beard before." She paused and then nodded her head. "I like it."

I returned her smile.

It was the first time Katherine had spoken to me since I'd tried to date her a couple of years ago.

Chapter 6

Katherine wasn't just an attractive woman; she was a beautiful woman. Whether it was her blond hair and green eyes or her fashion model figure, she had always commanded attention whenever she entered a room.

Although she wasn't shy about using her good looks to get attention, I'd quickly learned Katherine was more interested in receiving kudos for her analytical abilities than for her physical attributes.

"Thanks, Katherine," I said. "I've been looking forward to hearing what you've turned up on Amir Madani."

She opened up her laptop. "I was asked to expedite this request, so keep in mind these are only preliminary results."

"Don't be so modest, Katherine. You know you always do a thorough job."

She rewarded me with a smile. "And you always think flattery will get you quicker results."

Even though Katherine had given me the cold-shoulder after our short-lived relationship, we were still on good terms. While it was probably just wishful thinking on my part, I remained optimistic we might be able to reconnect one day.

Proximity was a huge factor in our break up—it's difficult to get close to someone when you're seldom in the same country, much less the same zip code together.

"Let's get started," Carlton said, picking up his Cross pen and scribbling something on his legal pad. When he looked up, he nodded at Katherine.

"Tell us what your data mining has turned up on Amir Madani."

Katherine glanced down at her laptop.

After reading off Amir Madani's full name, she said, "He appears to be a legitimate nuclear research scientist. We scanned his educational background and his employment history, and there were no red flags there. I also questioned the defector, Komeil Haddadi, about him. He said he'd met Madani once, but he couldn't offer much insight into his personality."

I added, "When Komeil showed me Amir's picture, he didn't give him high marks for his research."

Katherine looked amused. "He told me the same thing, but I suspect there might be a little intellectual jealousy going on with Komeil."

Carlton said, "Titus has verified Madani works at the Atomic Energy Building, and he's talked to sources in Tehran that back that up, so I'm not particularly concerned about the quality of Madani's research. Tell me about the source of his money. Is he on VEVAK's payroll?"

Katherine shook her head. "No, there's no evidence of that in our databases. That doesn't mean he's not being paid through one of their off-the-books accounts, but he's not on VEVAK's official payroll."

Carlton looked pleased. "What about Madani's bank records?"

She looked down at her computer again. "The year after Amir graduated from Tehran University, a substantial amount of money was deposited into a savings account he maintains at Maskan Bank of Tehran. It's possible those funds were from the sale of a piece of property owned by his father, who passed away before the property was sold. Keep in mind, though, it's a large sum of money for such a small piece of real estate, and I'm still trying to confirm if the sale could be the source of his money. A year after those funds appeared in his account, he purchased his apartment in Shemiran."

I said, "There's probably no need to ask you this, Katherine, but did you check the Nuclear Security Division's databases? Is there any evidence one of their operatives has ever tried to recruit him?"

She tucked a strand of hair behind her ear and gave me a dismissive look. "You're right, Titus. There's no need for you to ask me that." She paused. "Of course, I checked the NSD databases. There's nothing in there about Amir Madani."

Carlton looked amused at Katherine's answer and pointed his pen at me, "Any other questions?"

"No, I'm good."

Carlton turned to Katherine. "So what's your assessment?"

She closed the lid on her laptop. "I'll send you my full report tomorrow, but, as far as my office is concerned, Amir Madani appears to be a legitimate prospect for recruitment. There's no evidence he's working for VEVAK or for any other intelligence agency."

"That's good," Carlton said, running his hand over his baldhead. "That's very good."

Carlton appeared relieved, as if he might have been expecting bad news but had been given good news instead. His reaction made me wonder if he'd already alerted the DDO about the possibility of recruiting Amir. That would be out of character for my operations officer because he usually refused to divulge any new intel to the suits on the seventh floor until such information had been fully vetted.

However, if Carlton had gone against his cautious nature and told the DDO I'd recently been in contact with a nuclear scientist, then perhaps that meant he'd already asked the deputy to approve a change in status for Operation Torchlight.

Because of how the DDO felt about the lack of intel coming out of Iran, I assumed he would have immediately approved such a request.

It turned out I was wrong about that.

◆ ◆ ◆ ◆

After Carlton expressed his gratitude to Katherine for expediting his request, she assured him she would continue monitoring Madani's finances for any changes, and then she picked up her laptop and headed for the door.

Carlton quickly got out of his chair and opened the door for her. Before she left the room, she turned toward the video screen and gave me a little wave.

"Nice to see you again, Titus." she said. "Watch your back out there."

I nodded at her. "Always."

When Carlton sat back down, I said, "I think the best way for me to approach Madani—"

"Don't get ahead of yourself, Titus."

Carlton flipped through several pages of his legal pad. When he found the one he wanted, he said, "I realize this may surprise you, but this morning I took the unusual step of mentioning to Deputy Ira that you had recently met someone in Iran's nuclear community. I also expressed your willingness to add him to your network."

"You're right, Douglas," I said, trying to look sincere, "that does surprise me, especially since Katherine hadn't given you her results yet."

He looked off in the distance for a moment. "I had my reasons."

"I'm sure the DDO was excited to hear I might be able to recruit Madani."

He shook his head. "As a matter of fact, he wasn't. When I told him about your contact with Madani, he had a negative response."

I didn't have to fake my surprise this time. "Why?"

"I'll read his exact words to you," he said, looking down at his notes. "The deputy said, 'Titus already has his hands full managing six assets. If this scientist turns out to be a viable recruit, we'll send another operative into Iran to run him.'"

"Another operative? It would take at least six months for the Agency to insert another operative into Tehran. By that time, Madani could have already been feeding me intel."

Carlton laid his pen down beside his legal pad. After making sure the pen was precisely aligned with the top of the pad, he looked up at me and asked, "Are you absolutely certain Madani will respond to an approach from you?"

"No, Douglas, I'm not *absolutely* certain, but—"

"You just said—"

"I *am* certain I have a better chance of befriending Amir Madani than anyone else does. I've met the man. I have an opening there."

"You've never lacked for confidence, that's for sure."

"I have confidence Amir would like to become better acquainted with Hammid. He's curious about the watchmaker's son."

Carlton nodded. "Your instincts have usually been right about such things."

I waited, thinking he was going to qualify his statement, but, when he didn't, I said, "So you'll talk to the DDO again?"

"I already did. I assured him you could handle running another asset, and he finally agreed to amend the protocols for Operation Torchlight."

"Thank you for standing up for me, Douglas. I appreciate it."

"I didn't do it just for you," he said. "The Agency needs that intel."

After flipping a page over on his legal pad, Carlton asked, "How do you want to proceed with Madani?"

"First, I'll need an apartment in Shemiran."

He nodded. "By the end of the week, Hammid Salimi will hear from his parents in Geneva. They'll let him know they've purchased an apartment for him in Shemiran. Make sure he thanks them."

He did.

◆ ◆ ◆ ◆

I had to abandon my surveillance of Amir for a few days while I made arrangements for my move to Shemiran. Those arrangements included purchasing furniture for my new apartment.

One day, when I was on my way over to a furniture store, I got a text from Farid. He said he had a package for me, and he wanted to know how soon I could meet him.

I texted him back and told him I was tied up for a couple of hours, but I could meet him at the entrance to Jamshidieh Park at two o'clock.

I arrived at the park, located in northern Tehran not far from Shemiran, thirty minutes before our scheduled meet, which gave me plenty of time to scout out the area.

It was early afternoon, and, except for a few young mothers pushing baby strollers and some senior citizens playing checkers on a park bench, there was hardly anyone at the park.

When Farid arrived, I suggested we take one of the walking trails over to the tea house in the middle of the park. As soon as we headed over there, I mentioned I was moving to an apartment in Shemiran.

"You should hire Chaman's decorator to furnish it for you."

"Are you kidding?"

"No, I promise you won't regret it. You should see Chaman's apartment. It's very understated."

I hadn't told Farid about my visit to see his girlfriend, and, evidently, she'd failed to mention it to him as well.

"What do you mean Chaman's apartment is understated?" I said. "Since when do you know anything about decorating?"

He shrugged. "I'm just repeating what Chaman told me. She's been trying to convince me to hire her decorator to redo my own apartment."

"If Chaman's decorator is so good, why haven't you hired her?"

He smiled. "My father hates the way my apartment looks. Why should I change it?"

I shook my head. "Thanks anyway, but I'd rather do my own decorating."

When Farid began texting someone, I figured that was the end of our discussion, but, a few minutes later, he said, "I've just texted Chaman and asked her to meet us at the tea house. If you don't want to use her decorator, maybe she'll have another suggestion for you. I've been to your apartment, Hammid. Trust me, if you're going to live in Shemiran, you need a decorator."

I had more important things to discuss with Farid than decorating, so I didn't argue with him.

"Okay, sure," I said. "I'll look forward to hearing her suggestions." I pointed over to an empty park bench. "If Chaman's going to meet us at the tea house, we should do the exchange here."

As soon as we sat down, Farid pulled a manila envelope out of his jacket and handed it to me. "I found the video pretty boring. It's just two old men discussing the future of Iran. I could only stand to watch a few minutes of it."

I knew one of the old men Farid had seen in the video was the UN Secretary-General. During his recent visit to Iran, he'd stayed in the Parisian Asadi Hotel in downtown Tehran. As soon as he'd left Tehran, Carlton had instructed me to have Farid get a copy of the surveillance video from his room.

I asked Farid, "You didn't have any problem getting this, did you?"

He shook his head. "None. I told the hotel's security chief my father wanted the surveillance tapes from several rooms on that date. I've done this many times, and they've never questioned me about it. I'm sure they think I'm some kind of perverted voyeur."

After slipping the envelope containing the DVD inside my coat pocket, I pulled out another envelope—this one containing American dollars—and handed it to Farid.

Although he'd never turned down cash, I knew money wasn't his motivation for passing me intel. Like any good case officer, I also tried to ensure Farid's continuing cooperation by supplying him with the kind of motivation tailored specifically for him.

"I assure you, Farid, one day, when these videos are made public, your father will be disgraced."

He nodded. "I'm counting on that."

◆ ◆ ◆ ◆

Chaman arrived in the tea house about five minutes after Farid and I had been seated. When she breezed in the room, she looked every bit as beautiful as one of the models featured on the pages of *Afrand*, Iran's fashion magazine.

As required by the mullahs, Chaman was fully covered from head to toe, but her attire pushed the limits of what was considered acceptable clothing. Without a doubt, it bore little resemblance to the black chador worn by most Muslim women in the small Iranian towns outside of Tehran.

Her head covering, a bright orange headscarf, barely covered her dark brown hair and only drew attention to her heavily made-up eyes. She was also wearing a silky floral *manteau*, a long-sleeved, loose garment resembling a coat, and underneath the *manteau*, she had on a pair of dark trousers and a cream-colored blouse.

Farid and I both stood up and greeted her when she arrived.

After she was seated, she turned to me and said, "Hammid, I haven't seen you in ages."

"It's been awhile."

"How's your business? Have you enlisted any more investors?"

"A few."

"Anyone I know?"

"I don't believe so."

She lifted up the sleeve of her *manteau* and said, "See the present I bought for myself."

I smiled when I saw she was wearing a limited edition Salimi watch. "You made an excellent choice, Chaman. That watch is from our new Marit collection, and it suits you perfectly."

She admired it for a few minutes. "Yes, I thought so too."

After a waiter brought our order, Farid said, "Hammid purchased an apartment in Shemiran. You should give him the name of your decorator."

"In Shemiran?" she said. "That's not far from where I live."

"Really?" I said, playing her game. "Where do you live?"

"I'm in Shahre Tower on Maryam Street."

I nodded. "That's a nice neighborhood."

Chaman lifted her cup of steaming Chai tea to her lips and stared at me for a moment.

Once she'd taken a sip, she shook her head and said, "I'm sorry, Hammid. Until I've actually seen your apartment, I won't know which decorator I should choose for you."

Farid, who seemed oblivious to the flirtatious game Chaman was playing, said, "Shemiran is only twenty minutes away. When we're finished here, why don't we go see your apartment?"

Chaman smiled at me and said, "Yes, why don't we?"

Why not?

Chapter 7

The apartment the Agency had purchased for me in Shemiran was located in Building C, directly across the parking lot from Amir's apartment in Building B.

At first, I was disappointed when Carlton told me my apartment wasn't in the same building as Amir's, but when I realized one of the windows in my guest bedroom had a perfect view of the outside entrance to Amir's apartment building, then I changed my mind and decided Building C might be an ideal location after all.

When I showed Chaman and Farid my apartment, both of them commented on how roomy it was. Even though I agreed with them, I knew I'd be spending most of my time at the window in the guest bedroom scanning Amir's building with my binoculars.

"This is a great apartment," Farid said, opening up the empty refrigerator and looking inside. "I might have to move in here myself."

"Doesn't Amir Madani live in Shemiran?" Chaman asked Farid.

He nodded. "Yes, I believe so. When he spoke at the university, he mentioned that."

An innocent-looking smile played across Chaman's face when she looked over at me and asked, "Do you know Amir Madani?"

Chaman seemed to be having too much fun keeping secrets from Farid to drop her little conspiratorial drama, and I continued to indulge her.

"I met him a few weeks ago when Farid and I were having lunch at Zafaranieh Plaza."

Farid glanced down at his watch. "Speaking of Zafaranieh Plaza, they're holding a jacket for me at Versace. I should head over there before they close."

He leaned over and gave Chaman a demur peck on the cheek. "Choose a good decorator for Hammid. I promise you, he'll thank you for it later."

She laughed. "Oh, I plan to do everything I can for Hammid."

Farid shook his finger at me. "You should listen to her."

The moment Farid was out the door, I walked over to where Chaman was standing.

"What are you doing?" I asked, as she began removing the orange scarf from around her head.

She gave me a mischievous smile. "I'm taking off my headscarf. It's warm in here."

"You know that's not what I'm asking you."

"Then what *are* you asking me?"

"Why didn't you tell Farid I came by your apartment the other day?"

Chaman took a step closer to me. "Did you want me to tell him?"

"Do what suits you."

She reached over and placed both hands around my neck. As she touched her lips to mine, she said, "This is what suits me."

When I wrapped my arms around her and returned her kiss with more passion than she might have expected, she quickly stepped away from me.

Retrieving her headscarf, she said, "You won't be sorry if you let me hire my own decorator to furnish this apartment for you."

I shrugged. "Do what suits you."

◆ ◆ ◆ ◆

The next day, Chaman arrived at my apartment with her decorator in tow. She introduced her as Uzan. That was it. I wasn't given her last name. However, when I had the Ops Center check her out, I learned it was Darzi.

After I apologized to Chaman and Uzan for having nothing to offer them in the way of refreshments, Uzan asked me to describe my preference in decorating styles.

I tried not to laugh. "I'm not picky," I said. "All I ask is that you keep things simple."

"He doesn't really mean that," Chaman said, taking Uzan by the arm and leading her into the dining room.

Uzan swept her arm across the room. "This is *such* an elegant space," she said. "It needs to be furnished with lots of classical pieces."

Uzan used the Farsi word for classical that meant ornate, and I immediately envisioned her filling the room with handcrafted solid wood furniture adorned with elaborate carvings.

As I listening to her discussing her ideas with Chaman, it soon became apparent Uzan's services were about to cost the American taxpayers a boatload of cash.

I'd already purchased a chair—which Uzan told me she hated—so, while the two ladies wandered through the rooms, I sat down and began scripting out how I was going to explain my furniture expenses to Carlton.

Once they were finished touring my apartment, the ladies returned to the living room, where Uzan sketched out how she was envisioning each room.

After winding up her sales spiel, she said, "My main decorating goal will be to have each room reflect the exquisite tastes of the man who lives here."

I knew she couldn't possibly achieve that goal, but when she gave me her bottom line, I immediately agreed to let her decorate the place. When Chaman heard this, she looked both pleased and surprised.

Uzan just looked pleased.

I asked her, "Would you prefer to be paid in Iranian rials, Swiss francs, or American dollars?"

"My banker would prefer American dollars," she replied with a smile.

I nodded. "I'll make the arrangements."

I walked the ladies down the hall to the elevator.

Less than a minute after I returned to my apartment, I heard a knock on my door and found Chaman standing outside.

When I invited her in, she said, "I told Uzan I left my phone in here. She's waiting for me downstairs."

I glanced around the empty living room. "You didn't leave your phone in here."

"I know," she said with a smile. "It's in my purse."

"Why would you lie to her?"

She moved closer to me and ran her finger slowly down my cheek. "Isn't it obvious?"

I grabbed her hand. "You need to stop playing games, Chaman. I know you care about Farid."

She laughed. "Of course I care about Farid, but I also like playing games, if that's what you want to call this."

She caressed my lips with a soft kiss.

Before I had a chance to respond, she turned and walked out the door.

◆ ◆ ◆ ◆

For the next two weeks, I didn't have to make a decision about how I was going to handle Chaman.

Although Uzan and her crew were at my apartment every day, Chaman didn't make an appearance, and I used that time to consider what I should do about Farid's girlfriend before I found myself alone with her again.

While I wasn't about to let Chaman jeopardize my relationship with Farid, I decided I couldn't pass up an opportunity to use her reckless behavior to further my mission.

It was only after I experienced an unexpected encounter with Amir Madani that I realized how useful she might be to me.

◆ ◆ ◆ ◆

While Uzan and her crew were hanging draperies, moving in

furniture, and putting down carpet, I took refuge from the mayhem in the Viuna Café, a restaurant down the street from Shemiran.

I wasn't concerned about leaving the decorators alone in my new residence since all my personal possessions, including my Agency laptop and communication devices, were still at my old place.

Besides that, before Uzan and her crew had started working on the apartment, I'd installed pinhole cameras in every room.

Now, no matter where I was, I was able to watch everything the decorators were doing on my Agency sat phone. So far, it appeared they were doing nothing more than making my apartment look hideous.

I hadn't told Douglas Carlton about the cameras. If I had, he might have insisted I give the Ops Center their access codes.

I couldn't do that.

I wasn't about to allow the Agency to watch me 24/7.

They were already in my head enough as it was.

◆ ◆ ◆ ◆

One day, as I was walking back to my apartment from the restaurant, I spotted Amir Madani walking toward me. He was looking down at his mobile phone, and I wasn't sure he'd seen me.

For a moment, I considered slipping inside the doorway of a florist shop and avoiding him. But, since I'd been mapping out how I could manage to accidently run into him around the apartment complex, I made a quick decision and let the encounter play itself out as naturally as possible.

As we approached each other, he looked up and appeared to recognize me. I looked away for a moment, and then I did a double take and pretended to recognize him as well.

I stopped on the sidewalk in front of him and extended my hand. "It's Amir, isn't it?"

"That's right," he said, shaking my hand. Pointing toward the watch on my arm, he smiled and said, "Salimi watches."

I nodded. "Hammid Salimi. We met one day when I was having lunch with Farid Kazim in Zafaranieh Plaza."

"How is Farid? I haven't seen him in awhile."

"Neither have I. I've been busy moving into my new apartment." I pointed across the street. "I just bought a place in Shemiran. Well, actually, my parents bought it for me."

He looked surprised. "That's where I live. Which building are you in?"

"Building C. I'm up on the second floor."

"I'm just across from you in B. My apartment's also on the second floor. I wonder if we have the same floor plan."

"I'd invite you up for a cup of coffee, but my decorator's in there now, and I don't think she's ready for me to have guests yet."

"You hired a decorator?"

I laughed. "I was forced into it. After Farid saw the way I'd decorated my old apartment, he insisted I hire his girlfriend's decorator to furnish this one."

"His girlfriend? You mean Chaman Bijan?"

"That's right."

He smiled. "I'm surprised they're still together. When I met them at the university, they didn't seem that well suited for each other."

I nodded. "You're right. They don't share many interests."

"I was thinking more about their personalities. Chaman strikes me as someone who likes to challenge the status quo, and Farid seems content with the way things are."

"You're right about Farid, but I don't know Chaman all that well, except I can tell you, she wouldn't let me say no to her decorator."

He laughed. "Chaman is someone I wouldn't mind getting to know a little better. I like a woman with strong beliefs."

I gestured over at my apartment. "I promised Farid and Chaman I'd have them over for dinner as soon as I had a workable kitchen. Maybe you could join us."

He seemed startled by my invitation, which made me wonder if I was rushing things too much.

"Oh," he said, "I don't do much socializing. My work keeps me far too busy for that."

I smiled. "Everybody has to eat."

He pointed up the street at the Viuna Café. "Speaking of eating, that's where I was headed. I recommend it. It's the best restaurant in the neighborhood."

"I was just there myself."

As he started to walk away, he said, "Let me know when you get moved in. I'm in 205B."

Yes!

♦ ♦ ♦ ♦

I moved into my newly decorated apartment a week later, but I waited a few days before making contact with Amir. I wanted to see if he might decide to pay me a visit instead.

When that didn't happen, I began looking for an opportunity to show up at his doorstep, preferably, when he'd be forced to invite me inside.

One evening, after Amir had pulled his Mercedes into his garage, I saw him get out of his car carrying an armful of groceries. I figured that meant he planned to cook dinner for himself, and I saw that as the opportunity I'd been waiting for.

I gave him thirty minutes to start his meal, and then I walked across the parking lot, entered Building B, and took the elevator up to the second floor.

There was a brass doorknocker on the door of 205B, and, after tapping it a couple of times, I stepped back and waited for him to appear.

When he didn't come to the door after a minute or so, I knocked again. A peep hole was centered above the doorknocker, and, for a moment, I saw it darken, as if someone inside had looked through the fish-eye lens at me.

At that point, I fully expected Amir to open the door. When he didn't, I walked back down the hall to the elevator and pushed the button.

I wasn't sure what to make of Amir's behavior.

I had planned to invite him to have dinner with me at the Viuna Café, but since I figured the bag of groceries meant he was staying in and cooking for himself, I was hoping he might suggest we eat at his place instead.

From a tradecraft standpoint, that scenario would have been ideal. If a potential asset invited me inside their residence, the chances of recruiting that asset greatly increased. In fact, a potential asset seldom took the bait I offered them until that had happened.

If Amir's refusal to answer his door meant he wasn't interested in becoming friends with me, then my job had just gotten a whole lot harder.

When the elevator arrived on the second floor, I stepped aside to allow a young woman dressed in a dark blue *manteau* to exit the elevator. She smiled and lowered her head as she stepped in front of me.

Her pale-yellow headscarf had fallen down around her shoulders, and, after readjusting it, she turned and headed down the hallway in the direction of Amir's apartment. I held the elevator open long enough to see if 205B could possibly be her destination.

The moment I saw her lift the doorknocker to 205B, I stepped inside the elevator. Then, as the doors were closing, I heard Amir invite her inside.

He sounded happy to see her. I was pretty happy about it myself.

If I'd interpreted the situation correctly, Amir's reluctance to answer the door had nothing to do with me personally. It was simply a matter of him not wanting someone around when the young woman arrived at his place for dinner.

That was understandable.

Seeing the young woman at Amir's door made me more determined than ever to host a dinner party at my place and invite the nuclear scientist as one of my guests.

Naturally, I planned to invite Chaman as well.

◆ ◆ ◆ ◆

When I got back to my apartment, I sat down in front of the window in the guest bedroom and pointed my camera at the entrance to Building B. I planned to snap a few photographs of Amir's lady friend when she left the building and then upload them to the Ops Center for identification purposes.

However, as soon as my camera was positioned correctly, I spotted Farid pulling into a parking spot in front of my building.

Chaman was with him.

Since neither of them had seen the final results of Uzan's decorating efforts, I suspected the purpose of their impromptu visit was to critique the results.

For a moment, I considered not answering the door so I could capture some shots of the young woman. Then, I realized I couldn't do that because Farid had probably seen my car parked outside the building.

I immediately stashed my camera in a drawer in the guest bedroom and went to the door.

"I hope you don't mind," Farid said, when I invited them inside, "Chaman insisted we drop by."

"No, of course not."

As soon as Chaman greeted me, she walked over to a carved wooden cabinet, one that Uzan had described as being "the focal point of the room."

The cabinet was as wide as it was tall, and, as far as I could determine, it served no useful purpose whatsoever.

"This is perfect," Chaman said, running her hand across the inlaid surface. "I love the gold accents."

Chaman oohed and aahed her way around the living room, commenting on the gold tapestry couch and chairs, plus the mosaic coffee table.

Then, she entered the dining room.

"Exactly how I envisioned it," she said, sitting down in one of the gilded dining chairs.

When she stood up, she patted the red velvet cushion. "It's comfortable too."

As Chaman walked down the hall to inspect the bedrooms, Farid leaned over and whispered in my ear. "I hope you're not offended, Hammid, but, personally, I think Uzan overdid it."

PART TWO

Chapter 8

Tehran, Iran
November 21, 2014

In the following weeks, I managed to have several casual encounters with Amir. One time, I ran into him in the parking lot outside my building. A few days later, I followed him down the street to a local dry-cleaning establishment and entered it just as he was leaving.

On another occasion, I strolled up to a newspaper kiosk as he was purchasing a copy of *Kayhan*, one of Tehran's daily newspapers. After we exchanged greetings, I asked him if he'd like to go grab a cup of coffee with me. Although he made an excuse about running late for an appointment, he sounded sincere when he said he'd like to do it some other time.

Just before he walked off, I gave him my business card, and, a week later, he called me.

I was careful not to appear too eager when I accepted his invitation to try out a new restaurant.

During the meal, I only brought up his position at the Atomic Energy Building once. We spent most of the time discussing my background.

He seemed especially curious about my education, and I noticed he used the same type of interrogation technique I'd seen him use on

Farid when he was questioning him about Chaman.

I considered his interest in me a good thing, and, in an effort to get him to share something personal with me, when we were driving back to Shemiran, I voluntarily brought up some personal things about myself, including how much I enjoyed cooking.

He laughed when I told him about my hobby. "You hardly seem the type, Hammid."

Since cooking was considered a feminist trait in Iran, I immediately explained my culinary expertise was connected to my Swiss heritage, and I joked with him about keeping my pastime a secret.

I half-expected him to admit he wasn't averse to cooking himself, but his only response was to shrug and quote an old Persian proverb.

"An alive person needs life," he said.

After we arrived back at Shemiran, I decided it was time for me to take the next step in my recruitment of Amir. To that end, I issued him an invitation.

"I've invited a few friends to a dinner party at my place next week. Farid and Chaman plan to be there. Would you also be able to join us?"

Even though Amir didn't appear to be totally comfortable with me yet, he immediately accepted my invitation. "Sure, why not? I can't think of anything more enjoyable than arguing with Chaman for a few hours."

As I rode the elevator up to my apartment, I congratulated myself on my brilliant timing and my masterful plan to recruit Amir Madani.

Later, I had to revise my highly-overrated opinion of myself.

◆ ◆ ◆ ◆

Even before I opened the door to my apartment, I knew someone had paid me a visit while I was out having dinner with Amir.

Every time I left the building, I always set up at least one hidden trip marker, and when I checked the tiny plastic filament I'd placed across the door sill, I saw it had been triggered.

As soon as I discovered this, I removed my weapon from my

holster and slowly pushed open the door.

The moment I stepped inside the living room, I immediately caught a whiff of a masculine scent—something I couldn't identify, a kind of woodsy smell.

However, the living room was empty.

I walked down the hallway and checked out the other rooms.

Also empty.

I returned to the living room and took a look around.

That's when I spotted the overturned lamp.

It wasn't on the floor; it was leaning up against an armchair in a corner of the room. When Uzan had decorated my apartment, she'd placed a table lamp next to a high-backed chair. It was a chair she'd described as "perfect for reading." However, I'd quickly discovered the lamp was top-heavy and toppled over easily.

As I envisioned it, someone must have stepped behind the chair and tipped the lamp over without realizing it, or maybe they had stuck their hand behind the cushions and knocked the lamp over that way.

At any rate, they hadn't repositioned the lamp correctly.

Sloppy.

When I walked over to the antique wooden desk, I discovered the trip marker I'd placed under a stack of books had been moved, although the books themselves appeared undisturbed.

In spite of this, nothing in the apartment seemed to be missing.

It wasn't a robbery. The apartment had been searched; pure and simple.

For what purpose?

I pulled out my cell phone, sat down in my perfect-for-reading chair, and clicked on my security camera icon.

It was time to find out.

◆ ◆ ◆ ◆

When the archived video from the pinhole cameras in my apartment began appearing across my screen, the timeline showed two men entering my apartment approximately twenty minutes after Amir and I had pulled out of the parking lot at Shemiran.

One of the men had immediately headed back to the bedrooms, while the other guy had remained in the living room. Both men were dressed in casual attire. Both were wearing black leather half-boots with rubber soles and reinforced toes.

I had little doubt the two men were VEVAK agents. The search they conducted was methodical, quick, and professional.

There was only one problem with it.

Had I been asked to critique their technique during one of the periodic refresher courses at the Agency's training facility at Williamsburg, Virginia—better known as The Farm—I would have given the guy responsible for searching the living room lower marks for his failure to give the living room The Last Look.

The Last Look was a tenet of surveillance tradecraft drilled into all recruits at The Farm. It consisted of taking a moment before exiting the premises to survey the room. Had he done so, I'm sure he would have immediately spotted the overturned lamp.

Even so, I would have given both men high marks for their timing.

The search didn't take long. They were in and out of my apartment within thirty minutes.

Although I was concerned about what I'd just witnessed, I wasn't unduly alarmed by VEVAK paying me a visit because it appeared the men weren't looking for anything in particular. This was obvious when I observed the cursory way they'd looked through the drawers in the bedrooms and the cabinets in the kitchen.

VEVAK was notorious for such behavior. Iranians had no rights when it came to privacy and, unlike most Americans, they never imagined they did.

I felt sure what had triggered the search was Hammid Salimi's purchase of the apartment in the first place.

Even though Hammid was half-Iranian, he'd entered Iran on a Swiss passport. While his wealth made it less likely he could be the agent of a foreign power, I assumed the VEVAK officers had probably been told to check out the new tenant in Building C anyway.

Of course, it didn't escape my attention the apartment had been searched within a few minutes of my leaving Shemiran in the company of Amir Madani.

Was there a connection in the timing?

I didn't dismiss the idea entirely.

◆ ◆ ◆ ◆

I sent Carlton a text telling him we needed to talk, and he contacted me a few minutes later. I had no plans to tell him I'd captured the VEVAK agents on the video cameras I'd installed.

Before bringing up the search, I briefed him on my evening with Amir. His only comment—other than acknowledging the progress I was making—was to point out his concern about Amir's interest in my background.

"I'm troubled by the way he's probing your legend," he said. "Were these general questions he was asking you, or did he attempt to drill down a little further?"

"He usually followed up a general question with something more specific. After that, he would drop the subject entirely and circle back around to it later. He always admitted to bringing up the topic again, but then he would explain the redundancy by saying he needed more clarification about what I'd said earlier."

"Amir Madani sounds suspiciously like an interrogator to me."

"I understand why you'd think that, but he's also a trained research scientist. He's used to figuring out stuff by asking questions."

"That's something to consider."

After I told him about the dinner I was planning, I brought up the subject of my apartment being searched.

"One more thing, Douglas. While I was out with Amir, some unwelcomed guests showed up at my apartment. They let themselves in, took a look around, and left before I got home."

He was quiet for a moment.

"How obvious were they?"

"A couple of my markers were tripped, and they were sloppy. Nothing was missing; it wasn't a robbery."

"Probably local police. Of course, it could have been VEVAK."

"I'm leaning toward the latter."

"Why?"

"No reason. Just a gut feeling."

"If it happens again, you'll need to install cameras, audio, the whole works."

"Sure. If it happens again, I'll consider that."

VEVAK showed up again, but not at my apartment.

◆ ◆ ◆ ◆

A few days later, when I was on my way to meet Omid Askari, an Iranian banker who had been helping me funnel cash from the Agency to an Iranian opposition group, I spotted a tail.

The men shadowing me were driving a white Iranian Khodro, a knockoff Peugeot, the kind of vehicle driven by government workers, especially surveillance teams employed by VEVAK.

I was convinced it was VEVAK when I had a hard time losing the vehicle. Members of the local police force seldom received any kind of training in surveillance, and I felt sure if the occupants of the Khodro had been local policemen, then I would have been able to lose them just by making a few right turns.

On the other hand, the secret police had a division specifically schooled in surveillance tactics; losing them was a time-consuming process and involved lots of switchbacks.

It took me forty minutes to lose the VEVAK agents. Once that happened, as a precautionary measure, I immediately contacted Omid and put off our meeting.

◆ ◆ ◆ ◆

The next day, I spotted no sign of a tail, and when VEVAK didn't show up the day after that, I figured—much like the search of my apartment—it was a one-time surveillance assignment.

Then, the Khodro showed up again two days later.

This time when I spotted the VEVAK team, I'd just finished up a meeting with Fabel Reza. I suspected the VEVAK agents might have observed our encounter, and this was especially troubling because Reza was one of my most promising assets.

Although most of my assets had been recommended to me by Farid, that hadn't been the case with Fabel Reza.

I'd discovered Reza on my own by observing his behavior during a protest demonstration in Tohid Square following the election of the new president.

The protest organizers had been given all the necessary permits to conduct the demonstration, leading many Western journalists to speculate the government was using the protest as a propaganda tool to show the world the election was a democratic process.

They were right about that, of course.

While the protest was going on, I was inside a restaurant at a table next to a window. The window gave me a full, panoramic view of the crowd outside, and as I sat there studying the protesters, I happened to notice Reza.

He drew my interest because he didn't exhibit the same kind of enthusiasm for the protest as the rest of the participants did. Although he was carrying a placard, he didn't repeat the chants given to the protesters by the man with the loudspeaker, nor was he raising his fist or showing any other spontaneous response to the demonstration.

As the protest was breaking up, I saw Reza walk across the street and enter the crowded restaurant. When he began looking around for a table, I used the opportunity to wave him over to where I was seated.

"Would you care to join me?" I asked. "I'm almost finished here."

He hesitated. "Are you sure?"

"Positive." I glanced down at my watch. "I'm supposed to meet a client in twenty minutes."

As he sat down, he motioned out the window. "I hope you don't have far to go. There's still a crowd out there."

"I figure they'll be gone in a few minutes."

"What makes you think that?"

"Most of those protesters looked like university students. I imagine their professors told them it was their duty to come out to

Tohid Square today, and now, since they've fulfilled their obligation, they'll be eager to spend the rest of the day pursuing more entertaining activities."

"Are you sure about that?" he asked, pointing to the placard he'd carried into the restaurant. "I'm not a student, and I was out there protesting."

I made a show of looking him over for a moment.

He appeared to be around thirty years old, short haircut, neatly trimmed beard, an able-bodied man. Even so, he didn't have a military bearing, so I knew he wasn't a soldier, nor was he dressed like a bureaucrat. His clothes were clean, but of poor quality.

Finally, I said, "I'm guessing you were one of the paid protesters."

He looked down at his feet for a second. When he looked up, he nodded. "You're right. How did you know that?"

I spun him a yarn and told him I was a student of human nature and studying people was a hobby of mine. Then, I pointed out a couple of people in the square and made up a short story about them.

"What about him?" he asked, pointing to well-dressed man about to cross the street.

"Your turn," I said. "What's his profession? How old is he? Where's he headed now?"

His analysis of the man was surprisingly close to mine. "Are you also a student of human nature?" I asked. "On second thought, let me guess. You have a good imagination, so I'll bet you're a writer."

He nodded. "I suppose you could say that. I write my own songs." He stuck out his hand. "Fabel Reza."

"Hammid Salimi," I said, shaking his hand. "I'm a salesman, mostly watches. Are you a professional musician?"

"If you mean do I get paid for writing music, the answer is yes, but if you mean do I make a living with my music, the answer is no." He pointed down at the placard. "I occasionally have to supplement my income by getting paid to do other things."

There was something about Reza that struck a chord with me, and I made a quick decision—something I seldom did—and asked him if he'd be interested in making some deliveries for me. I explained the work would be sporadic, but when I told him how many Iranian rials I'd pay him to deliver a watch to a client, he immediately took me up on my offer.

In the months that followed, I discovered Reza had strong views about Iran's nuclear program, and he was adamantly opposed to the mullah's efforts to obtain a nuclear weapon. The more I encouraged him to explain his opposition to the regime, the more I realized it would be easy for me to recruit him as an asset.

Unfortunately, Reza was not wealthy, and he was unable to help the opposition with their funding needs, nor did he have access to anyone who might have intel that would be helpful to the opposition.

According to Carlton, Reza's shortcomings precluded his recruitment, and I wasn't given permission to pursue him as an asset for the mission of Operation Torchlight.

All that changed a month later when Reza landed a job at a bookstore frequented by members of the Iranian Parliament.

The bookstore was located around the corner from the legislative offices and featured a coffee shop that had live entertainment during the evening hours. Reza was hired to work part-time as a waiter and then to provide the patrons with entertainment at night.

When I visited the bookstore and saw how often he engaged the legislators in conversation, and how popular his original songs were with the clientele, I decided to approach Carlton again about recruiting him.

This time, he approved my request.

As expected, my recruitment of Reza was not difficult, and it wasn't long before he was providing the Agency with bits and pieces of intel on various members of the Iranian Parliament.

Reza was a natural when it came to picking up tradecraft—unlike Farid—and I used our weekly meetings to help him hone his skills at asking questions and reading body language.

Now, when I realized the two VEVAK agents were shadowing me, I decided the next time I met up with Reza, I would need to teach him how to spot a tail.

Unfortunately, there would be no next time.

Chapter 9

Tehran, Iran
December 12, 2014

When I told Farid and Chaman I was having a dinner party at my apartment and inviting some of my neighbors, Chaman immediately asked me if I had invited Amir Madani.

"Yes, I did," I said, "and when I told him I was planning to invite you and Farid, he said he was looking forward to seeing you again."

"Is that right?" she asked with a playful smile. "I wonder if he meant it."

"Of course he meant it," I said. "He specifically mentioned how much he enjoyed the candid way you challenged his views the last time he saw you."

Farid, Chaman, and I were standing in the lobby of the Iranshahr Theater, one of the oldest theaters in Tehran. It was during the intermission of "Green Orange," a play by a popular Iranian theater troupe.

Farid's father had a box seat at the theater, and when Farid had invited me to the production, I'd seen it as an opportunity to meet up with one of my assets.

The asset's name was Hosein Jamali. He was the owner of a jewelry store in Tehran whose clientele included the wives of some of the top generals in the Iranian Revolutionary Guard Corps (IRGC).

When we'd first arrived at the theater, I'd briefly encountered Jamali in the hallway outside our box and slipped him an envelope full of American dollars. In turn, he'd handed me a list of the banks where the IRGC generals had their money stashed, along with their corresponding account numbers.

Now, I was trying to think of an excuse to leave the theater during the intermission, so I could send the list to the Ops Center.

"Who's catering your dinner party?" Farid asked.

"No one," I said. "I'm doing my own cooking."

"You should at least hire someone to serve the food," Chaman said. "Otherwise, you won't be able to enjoy your guests."

"She's right," Farid said. He grabbed his cell phone out of his pocket. "I'll asked our restaurant manager if he could recommend someone to help you."

Before I could stop him, Farid walked over to a corner of the lobby to make his call.

When Chaman saw he was out of earshot, she leaned in toward me and asked, "Will you invite a date to your dinner party?"

"I'm not sure. Perhaps."

"Farid told me you were seeing Aviz Davar. Is she the type of woman you find appealing?"

Not long after Farid had agreed to work for the Agency, I'd asked him to introduce me to any of his friends who had expressed an interest in the Iranian dissident movement. A few months later, he'd introduced me to Aviz Davar.

Ironically, Aviz was the daughter of Colonel Davar of the IRGC, who was in charge of monitoring the activity of Iranian dissidents.

After our Agency analysts had probed her background, Carlton had suggested I pursue Aviz as a love interest in order to get her to feed me intel on the colonel.

It wasn't long before I realized nothing romantic was ever going to happen between Aviz and me. Any overture I made in that regard was quickly rebuffed.

However, one day, when Aviz and I were having dinner together, I expressed empathy for a dissident who had recently been arrested. She happened to know the background of his arrest, and, as she told me about him, tears came to her eyes.

It was then I realized the best way to connect with Aviz was on an emotional level.

That's how she primarily related to people. A hurt child, a severely handicapped man, a dog with only three legs, any kind of suffering, immediately brought tears to her eyes.

Like most men, I didn't find it easy to express my emotions, and I'd never enjoyed being around a woman who was highly emotional.

Nevertheless, the more outrage I expressed at the beating of a protester or the more sympathy I showed at the imprisonment of a Christian pastor, the closer Aviz and I became.

It wasn't long before Aviz took the bait I dangled in front of her. After that, as long as I assured her the tidbits of information she was passing on to me would lessen the suffering of the dissidents, she willingly handed over any information she was able to pick up from her father about the enemies of the regime.

"Yes," I told Chaman. "Aviz is exactly the type of woman I find appealing."

Chaman glanced over at Farid, who was making his way back over to us. "I don't believe you," she said.

Farid handed me a slip of paper he'd torn off his program. "The manager recommended you contact one of these people to help you with your dinner party. He said they're in high demand, so you should probably get in touch with them right away."

As I took the slip of paper from him, I glanced down at my watch. "It's not too late to call them this evening. If you'll forgive me, I'll slip out and do that now."

Farid waved me off. "Sure; go ahead."

"I forgive you," Chaman said with a smile.

♦ ♦ ♦ ♦

Although I told Amir my love of cooking was the result of my Swiss heritage, in reality, I'd learn to cook by spending time in the kitchen with my mother when I was growing up in Flint, Michigan.

I'd spent most of that time at the kitchen table doing my homework and fighting with my sister, Carla, but, along the way, I'd picked up the basics of how to prepare a few meals.

Now, I usually volunteered to do the cooking when I was stuck in a safe house with a bunch of other operatives. Mostly, I did this just to pass the time, but sometimes I did it to give myself a little taste of home.

Although I'd never mentioned my cooking abilities to Carlton, somehow, he'd found out about them, and, in the fall of 2010, after I'd returned from an assignment in Beirut, he told me the Agency had enrolled me in the L'Academie de Cuisine Culinary School in Gaithersburg, Maryland.

This was a crash course to prepare me for an operation in Dubai, United Arab Emirates, where I was to pose as an Executive Chef at the Dubai International Hotel. The training only lasted for two weeks, but it was enough to get me the job when the American chef in the hotel's restaurant mysteriously came down with a case of food poisoning.

I was sent to Dubai because a resident of the hotel, Asad Badawi, was laundering money for Al-Qaeda, and my assignment was to install a software program on his laptop in order to monitor all his banking transactions.

Badawi loved American cuisine, and, one day, after I'd delivered a meal up to his suite on the tenth floor, I was able to complete my assignment.

Not only was the operation a success, I also added a few new recipes to my cooking repertoire during the mission.

For obvious reasons, I had no plans to have any American dishes on my menu for my dinner party with Amir Madani. Instead, I was planning to serve my guests traditional Iranian dishes.

However, the day before my dinner party, I came across a vendor selling broccoli at one of the farmers' markets, and in an effort to make an impression on Madani, I added it to my menu.

When we'd eaten at the restaurant together, Madani had mentioned he'd tasted broccoli for the first time at a London hotel during a nuclear energy conference. He said he found the vegetable delicious, but he hadn't been able to find a restaurant in Tehran that served it.

I wasn't a big fan of broccoli, but I remembered liking a broccoli dish my mother used to serve at Thanksgiving, which was basically cooked broccoli smothered in a ton of butter and cheese, so I decided to give the dish a Swiss name, *brokkoli cremig*, and serve it to my guests.

I didn't really expect the broccoli to be a deciding factor in my recruitment of Madani, but, in the game of espionage, I never knew if a cruciferous vegetable might put one in the win column for our side.

◆ ◆ ◆ ◆

The antique dining table Uzan had purchased for my apartment seated twelve people, and I had invited eleven guests.

Besides Amir Madani, my guest list primarily consisted of some of my clients, a few of the other occupants of my building, and, of course, Farid and Chaman.

To make sure there was an even number of men and women, I'd included two sisters who lived in my building, since Madani had told me he wouldn't be bringing a date, and, contrary to what I'd told Chaman, I had no intention of inviting Aviz Davar.

As soon as my guests began arriving, I gave Ahmad, the server I'd hired for the evening, a few last words of instructions and left the kitchen in his hands.

The two sisters who lived down the hall were the first ones to show up at my door. Like all of my guests, they didn't arrive empty-handed. By the time Amir Madani appeared, I'd already been showered with two boxes of Iranian chocolates, a tin of nuts, and some pastries from a local bakery.

Strangely enough, Madani chose to bring me a box of dark chocolate truffles from Teuscher's, the famous Swiss chocolatier.

I thanked him profusely.

Farid and Chaman arrived fashionably late. Once I'd introduced them to everyone, I invited my guests to the dining room, where I'd already placed name cards at each place setting.

Naturally, I'd seated Amir next to Chaman.

Before long, they were engaged in a lively discussion that excluded everyone else in the room.

That changed as soon as Ahmad served the *brokkoli cremig*. When Madani tasted it, he looked over at me and said, "Hammid, now I have proof you've been lying to me about who you really are."

Even though his statement took me off guard, I smiled and said, "Why would you say that, Amir?"

"You said your mother is Swiss, right?"

"That's right."

"And you said she's in the jewelry business, right?"

I nodded.

He shook his head. "You must be lying about that. Only a Swiss chef could make such a delicious dish."

I relaxed.

◆ ◆ ◆ ◆

By the time the dessert was served, I could tell Farid was frustrated by the way Chaman was ignoring him and devoting all her attention to Amir.

The younger of the two sisters was seated to the left of Farid, and, in an obvious move to make Chaman jealous, he began flirting with her.

Farid's actions didn't go unnoticed by Chaman.

Instead of ignoring him and continuing to bewitch Amir with her charms—as I suspected she might—she immediately attempted to bring Farid into their conversation.

"Farid," she said, "you must tell your joke about the Iranian grandma who wanted to become an Israeli citizen."

Farid, who was a great storyteller, seemed pleased at her request, and he immediately began describing the grandma, the Israeli bureaucrat, and the circumstances surrounding the grandma's request to become an Israeli citizen.

When he finally delivered the punch line, everyone around the table burst out laughing.

Although Amir politely joined in the laughter, he didn't seem amused when Chaman encouraged Farid to tell another joke. Then, as the evening wore on, and Chaman brushed off Amir's attempts to reengage her in conversation, Amir turned his attention to me.

"Will your parents be coming to see your new apartment, Hammid?" he asked.

"I don't expect them to visit anytime soon. This is a busy time of year for them."

"But surely they would want to see where their son is living in Tehran. And what about your father, wouldn't he want to visit his homeland?"

Once again, I began fielding questions from Amir about my background.

This time, however, his interrogation set off some alarm bells.

A few days later, the sirens began to wail.

PART THREE

Chapter 10

Tehran, Iran
December 20, 2014

A few days after my party, I initiated a video call with the Ops Center to transmit some intel I'd received from Omid. I also wanted to give Carlton a brief rundown on what I'd observed about Amir during my dinner party.

Once Carlton gave me kudos on the progress I was making in getting closer to Amir Madani, I decided not to mention the man's continued interest in my background. I rationalized my decision by telling myself I needed to put Amir under surveillance again before informing my handler I suspected he might be gathering intel on me instead of vice versa.

However, I knew that was only partially true.

In the back of my mind, I realized I was reluctant to tell Carlton about my suspicions because I didn't want to admit I could have been wrong about Amir.

A couple of days after I began shadowing Amir again, Carlton notified me he had an urgent assignment for Farid, one involving the International Atomic Energy Agency (IAEA).

The IAEA was sending a delegation to Tehran to visit Iran's nuclear facilities in order to assess whether they were in compliance with the new UN resolutions regarding Iran's nuclear program.

The Agency had learned the IAEA delegation would be staying at the Asadi Hotel in downtown Tehran, and I was instructed to have Farid obtain the surveillance videos from their hotel rooms.

When I called Farid to set up a meeting, he suggested we meet outside the Imamzadeh Mosque on Darya Boulevard near his apartment. He said he planned to attend noonday prayers at the mosque.

Since Farid was not a devoted Islamist and seldom attended the mosque except on holy days, I wondered what had prompted his desire to be at the prayer service.

I arrived at the mosque thirty minutes before our scheduled meeting. After doing a careful recon of the area, I slipped inside.

The service was already in progress, and, as I sat there on a colorful Persian rug listening to the mullah deliver his sermon, I surveyed the room to see if I could locate Farid among the hundreds of men in attendance.

I finally spotted him sitting close to the front, near the end of the second row. As he gazed up at the mullah, he appeared mesmerized by the words coming out of his mouth.

The cleric was explaining *Sura* 16:129 from the Quran, *"Allah is with those who are righteous and those who do good."*

During other assignments, I'd had to memorize several chapters or *suras* from the Quran, but this *sura* wasn't one I recognized. Even if I had, I doubt if it would have had much impact on me.

I wasn't a religious person.

I wasn't opposed to someone worshipping a Higher Power, Buddha, Allah, God, or some other deity, but I'd seen little practical benefit from it. In my mind, religion brought the world a lot more misery than it did joy.

When the service finally ended, and the men began filing out of the mosque, I managed to fall into step alongside Farid. As we walked into the outer courtyard together, I suggested we go across the street and have lunch at an Indian restaurant called Cingari.

After the waiter took our order, I asked Farid, "What made you decide to attend prayers at the mosque today?"

He gave me a somber look. "I wanted to fulfill my obligations to

Almighty Allah before I die."

Although I was stunned by his response, I tried not to show it.

"You make it sound like your death is imminent."

"I believe it is."

◆ ◆ ◆ ◆

My first thought was that Farid's father had discovered his son was spying on his hotel guests and was threatening to kill him.

"What makes you think you're about to die?"

"I had a dream last night," he said, "but it wasn't like any dream I've ever had before. I was sitting in a chair in an empty room and standing beside me was a man dressed all in black with a sword in his hand. He kept asking me over and over again why I didn't deserve to die, and I didn't have an answer for him."

I felt an immediate sense of relief. "You had a dream, Farid. It wasn't a window into your future."

"You don't know that."

There was nothing I could say to convince Farid he wasn't going to die anytime soon, but after I told him about his new assignment, he dropped the subject and assured me he would have no trouble obtaining the surveillance videos from the hotel rooms of the IAEA inspectors.

Before we left the restaurant, Farid agreed to meet me at Assar Art Gallery on Barforooshan Street in downtown Tehran in three days.

Three days later, when Farid didn't show up for our appointment, I got worried.

◆ ◆ ◆ ◆

It wasn't unusual for Farid to occasionally miss an appointment. What *was* unusual was for him not to call me and let me know he wasn't going to be able to meet me for one reason or another.

After I wandered around the art gallery for an hour, I tried phoning him.

My call went to voice mail.

Thirty minutes later, I tried texting him.

He didn't reply.

Finally, I decided to stop by his apartment.

As soon as I got off Azadegan Expressway—the outer loop around Tehran—I realized my watchers in the white Khodro were back on the job.

I decided it was not to be, and I abandoned my plans to contact Farid until the next day.

◆ ◆ ◆ ◆

The next morning, when Farid still wasn't responding to my attempts to contact him, I managed to lose the VEVAK agents parked outside my building and drive over to Farid's neighborhood.

His apartment building had an underground parking facility manned by a security guard, who was seated inside a glass-enclosed booth. I sat across the street and watched the booth for almost an hour, as I tried to figure out how to get inside the garage without being seen.

The first thing I noticed was that the guard had a boring job.

He tried to pass the time by watching a small screen television set mounted above his head. It was daytime programming, which, in Iran, mainly consisted of news stories, clips of IRGC military exercises, and broadcasts of sermons from well-known Imams. None of it appeared to hold the guard's attention for any length of time.

However, it wasn't long before I detected a pattern behind his television viewing, and the next time he flipped the channel over to a news program—something he appeared more interested in than anything else—I got out of my car and ambled down the sidewalk in front of the building.

When I arrived at the booth, the guard was facing away from me watching his tiny television.

He appeared completely distracted by a news story about the Syrian Air Force using chemical weapons on a rebel stronghold, and I managed to slip underneath the guard rail and descend the short incline into the darkened parking garage before he saw me.

When I arrived at Farid's assigned parking space, I found it empty. I considered that a good sign.

More than likely, Farid had decided to take a trip and had forgotten to cancel our appointment. Since cell phone service was notoriously spotty in the Iranian countryside, I figured this was a real possibility.

Of course, there were several other possibilities, including his being arrested by VEVAK, but since I'd seen no evidence anyone besides the security guard was watching Farid's apartment building, I didn't believe anything like that had happened.

When VEVAK arrested someone, they usually set up surveillance around the person's residence immediately. Then, when friends or family members showed up to check on the missing person, they also took them into custody. It was a much more efficient method than broadcasting someone's arrest and then scouring the countryside looking for the acquaintances of the accused.

Although I told myself Farid had probably gone out of town, and his disappearance didn't have anything to do with his espionage activities, I knew there was no way I could be sure of that without checking out his apartment.

However, if I was wrong, and VEVAK had indeed arrested Farid, then showing up at his front door could prove detrimental to my well-being.

With that in mind, I removed my Glock from my holster before taking the elevator up to the fifth floor.

◆ ◆ ◆ ◆

Farid's apartment took up the entire fifth floor of the building. His father had purchased the five-story apartment building the day after Farid had graduated from Tehran University, and then he'd remodeled what had once been three separate apartments into one large residence for his son.

Even though the public elevator still permitted access to the fifth floor, a visitor was only allowed to enter a wood-paneled foyer outside Farid's front door. After that, a security code had to be entered on the keypad attached to the doorframe, or someone inside the apartment had to unlock the door after observing the visitor through an overhead camera.

I wasn't concerned about getting inside the apartment.

What concerned me was whether VEVAK had stationed its agents in the foyer outside Farid's front door.

While I could have taken the stairs at the back of the apartment and avoided the foyer altogether, the narrow stairwell would have been a kill zone in the event of a firefight between me and VEVAK's agents.

As I watched the numbers on the control panel tick off each passing floor, I held my gun at my side and pressed my back up against the inside corner of the elevator, trying to make myself as small a target as possible.

When the doors slid open on the fifth floor, I stayed out of sight, while keeping my thumb pressed against the elevator's open door button on the console.

Nothing happened.

No one stuck their head in the door to find out why an empty elevator had arrived on the fifth floor.

◆ ◆ ◆ ◆

Once I stepped off the elevator, I immediately walked over and looked up at the security camera installed above the door. To make sure the camera was capturing a good shot of me, I kept my face tilted toward the camera when I rang the doorbell.

No one came to the door.

I waited another thirty seconds and rang the bell a second time; still no response.

Finally, I keyed in Farid's numeric code on the security panel, and after hearing the lock release, I turned the door handle and entered the apartment.

Everything looked normal inside—normal, that is, for Farid.

Chaman had once referred to Farid's apartment as "a perfect

example of minimalist chic." In Farid's case, this primarily consisted of black and white furnishings with a minimum of color, plus lots of chrome and glass.

His father hated it. I wasn't too fond of it myself.

After checking out the front of the apartment, I walked back to Farid's bedroom, where I hoped to find some evidence he'd decided to go away for a few days.

Because of his extensive wardrobe, it was hard to tell if any of Farid's clothes were missing, but after I spotted two suitcases on the top shelf, I began to suspect he hadn't left town after all.

My doubts were confirmed when I checked out his bathroom. There, I found his toothbrush and various hair products scattered across the counter as if he'd just finished using them. I also discovered his toiletry kit stowed underneath the sink.

Now, the possibility that Farid had taken a vacation seemed remote.

◆ ◆ ◆ ◆

I walked across the hall to Farid's study. The only books on the shelves of the built-in bookcases were some of Farid's old textbooks from his student days at Tehran University.

Farid wasn't much of a reader.

However, his lack of literary interest was overshadowed by his passion for high-tech computer equipment. This obsession was reflected in the expensive computer sitting atop his black wooden desk and the two wide-screen monitors beside it.

I bent down and took a closer look at the screen on the right, where Farid's personal calendar and the previous day's appointments were displayed.

In the three o'clock time slot, Farid had entered "Meet H.S. at Assar Gallery." Presumably, those initials stood for Hammid Salimi.

The only other appointment on Farid's calendar was at noon. "Lunch with Chaman. Meet at Gilaneh."

Had Farid also missed his lunch with Chaman yesterday?

There was only one way to find out.

Chapter 11

As soon as I left Farid's apartment, I phoned Chaman and asked her to meet me at Jamshidieh Park. On my way over to the park, I contacted two of Farid's friends, both of whom had purchased Salimi watches from me.

Although I said I was calling to see how they were enjoying their new timepieces, before I hung up, I brought up Farid's name. When I asked if they'd heard from him recently, one of the men said he'd talked to Farid three days ago, and the other one said he hadn't seen Farid in a week.

I was hoping Chaman might be more helpful.

She'd agreed to meet me in Jamshidieh Park in front of a statue of Abolqasem Ferdowsi. Ferdowsi was a famous Iranian poet who was venerated throughout Iran. Statues of him were everywhere in the city, and I suspected every Iranian family owned at least one copy of his epic poem, *Shahnameh*.

I'd even seen a copy of *Shahnameh* on Farid's bookshelf.

However, it wasn't until I arrived at the park for my rendezvous with Chaman, that I realized I'd probably chosen the Ferdowsi statue on a subconscious level.

Since every biographer of Ferdowsi always included the story of how Ferdowsi's girlfriend had refused to give him shelter when his enemies were trying to kill him, perhaps I'd associated the poet's life with Farid.

◆ ◆ ◆ ◆

When Chaman arrived, I wasn't at the statue. I was watching her from a grove of trees near the children's playground about fifty yards away.

As soon as I was able to determine she wasn't being followed, I walked over and sat down beside her on a wooden park bench.

"Oh, Hammid, you startled me," she said, shaking her head. "Why did you sneak up on me like that?"

"I'm sorry, Chaman. I thought you heard me."

"I didn't hear you."

"I apologize."

"Maybe I'm just nervous because of what happened to Farid."

"What happened to Farid?"

"You don't know? I thought that's why you wanted to see me."

"That *is* why I wanted to see you. He was supposed to meet me yesterday, but I haven't heard from him, and he hasn't returned my calls."

She pulled her *manteau* closer to her as if she were chilled. "I'm sure it's nothing, but when we were having lunch yesterday at Gilaneh, two men approached our table and asked to speak to Farid privately. When the three of them returned a few minutes later, Farid told me he was under arrest."

"Who were these men?"

"They weren't wearing uniforms, and I didn't see any kind of identification on their vehicle."

"You followed them outside?"

She nodded. "I kept shouting at them, trying to tell them Farid hadn't done anything wrong." She shook her head. "I'm sure everyone in the restaurant heard me."

"I'm surprised they didn't arrest you."

"I wasn't worried," she said, brushing aside my remark with a flick of her hand.

"What kind of vehicle were they driving?"

"It was white. I believe it was a Khodro."

◆ ◆ ◆ ◆

After Chaman told me about the car, I knew Farid was in trouble. Depending on the type of interrogators VEVAK used and the amount of evidence they had on Farid, that trouble might eventually affect me and the rest of my network.

Now, I had no choice but to get in touch with Carlton and alert each of my assets to the danger Farid's arrest posed to them.

First, though, I had to get away from Chaman.

"I'm not worried about Farid," I said. "He can talk his way out of anything."

She didn't look all that convinced, but she nodded her head anyway. "As soon as I find out where they've taken him, I'm going to call some of my activist friends and organize a protest. Would you like to join us?"

I lied and said, "Sure, but Farid will probably be released before that happens."

I glanced down at my watch. "Listen, Chaman, I need to go meet a client now, but I'll call you later to see if you've heard from him."

She seemed surprised. "You're leaving?" She gestured in the direction of the tea house. "I thought we might have lunch together."

"No, I'm sorry," I said, getting to my feet. "I can't do that today."

As I walked away, I glanced back over my shoulder and waved at her.

I knew I'd probably never see her again.

◆ ◆ ◆ ◆

As soon as I got back to my car, I sent a text to each of my other assets asking them to contact me, and then I drove over to my apartment and called Carlton.

"Are you saying VEVAK has had Farid in custody for over twenty-four hours now?" Carlton asked.

"That's right."

"And you didn't spot any surveillance at his apartment?"

"None. Maybe they're just harassing him."

"Is that just wishful thinking on your part, or do you have some basis for believing that?"

"Farid doesn't have a good reputation in Islamic circles. He drives flashy cars and wears expensive clothes, and he seldom attends the mosque. Usually, when such undisciplined behavior is brought to the attention of the mullahs, they take some kind of action."

"That's true, but I've never heard of the mullahs using VEVAK to teach the nonobservant a lesson."

"Neither have I."

Carlton was quiet for a moment. "I have to assume you've already contacted your other assets?"

"Yes, but I haven't heard back from them yet."

"Not even Omid?"

The banker, Omid Askari, was the oldest of my assets and the most responsive when it came to answering my texts or agreeing to meet with me.

"I don't expect to hear from Omid Askari anytime soon. He's taken his family to a resort on the Caspian Sea and more than likely, he's out of cell phone range."

"What's your assessment? What does your gut tell you?"

"As much as I hate to do it, I believe I need to go to ground for a few days."

"I agree. Do that and then contact me the minute you hear from your other assets. In the meantime, I'll get the Ops Center to see what they can find out about Farid's arrest."

After I told Carlton I'd be leaving my apartment in the next fifteen minutes, he said, "Go ahead and turn on your tracker, Titus. I want you on The Grid until further notice."

Once I got off the phone with Carlton, I packed a carryall with my shaving kit, a couple of changes of clothing, my laptop, and some extra ammo, and then I walked out of my apartment.

Before pulling out of the Shemiran parking lot, I entered my three-digit code on my Agency sat phone. Now, my location was a pulsating blue dot on the Schematic Tracking Grid in the Ops Center at Langley. If Farid's arrest turned out to be nothing more than the mullahs giving him a slap on the wrist, then my blue dot on The Grid would keep on pulsating.

If not, at least the Ops Center would have a record of my last known location.

◆ ◆ ◆ ◆

When I'd arrived in Iran two years ago, I'd rented a one-bedroom apartment in the Avini district, a lower income neighborhood in Tehran. The lease was under the name of Malik Nasir.

For the last two years, I'd been paying rent on the apartment for six months at a time. Occasionally, I'd even put in an appearance at the place. While I always hoped I'd never have to use the safe house, it was there in case I did.

Now, I did.

After leaving Shemiran, I drove over to the Avini apartment and deposited my carryall, along with my laptop. Then, I grabbed the identity papers for Malik Nasir and caught a taxi to a car rental place near the airport, where I rented an older model Renault.

Since none of my assets had returned the phone messages I'd left them, there was nothing left to do but go check on them in person.

The jewelry store owned by Hosein Jamali was in a high-end shopping district on the outskirts of Tehran, not far from the airport, and I decided to make Jamali's jewelry store my first stop.

However, as I drove down the street in front of the store, I got caught up in a traffic jam. Traffic had come to a complete stop about a block from my destination, and, like most of the other drivers, I got out of my vehicle and began asking the pedestrians coming from that direction what was happening up ahead.

"There's been a terrible accident," one of them said. "A truck hit an old man crossing the street. I'm sure he's dead."

When traffic started moving again, I got back inside the Renault, but, for some reason, the closer I got to the accident's location, the more apprehensive I became.

VEVAK's modus operandi, particularly when dealing with enemies of the state, wasn't always predictable. Sometimes, they arrested the person, gave them a warning, and then immediately released them. At other times, the offender was executed by firing squad within twenty-four hours of his arrest.

The secret police had also been known to murder an enemy outright, especially if the evidence against them had come from a reliable source, and they didn't want to spend the time and resources on an investigation.

Since Hosein Jamali was a friend of several of the IRGC generals, I feared VEVAK might have chosen to stage some sort of accident instead of arresting him, thus preventing their actions from coming under the scrutiny of the IRGC.

When the line of traffic finally reached the accident site, my worst fears were realized.

Unlike what usually happens in other countries when a victim dies at the scene of a traffic accident, in Iran, the body wasn't always covered up immediately—I always figured the regime wanted onlookers to confront death in all its messy reality.

As I viewed the exposed body from my car window, I immediately knew the victim I saw lying in the street was Hosein Jamali. Although Jamali's chest and lower extremities had been crushed by the oncoming truck, his face was instantly recognizable.

I quickly looked away and moved on.

◆ ◆ ◆ ◆

As I drove over to Tehran University to check on Bahram Rouhani, a political science professor who had been feeding me intel on one of the dissident groups in Iran, I received a text from Aviz Davar.

The text was short but reassuring. *"I'll call you later. I'm off to swim now."*

Aviz swam at least three days a week at the Vanak Recreational Center, a members only facility. She was extremely regimented about her exercise routine, and I knew if I texted her back and asked her to call me, she'd wait until she'd finished her swim to get back to me.

Because the Vanak Center controlled access to the facility through a security guard, I felt certain Aviz was safe from VEVAK's reach—at least for now.

However, I decided after I had visited with the professor and explained the precautions he should take, I'd drive over to the Vanak Center and try to convince Aviz to go with me to the safe house.

When I arrived at the university and began making my way over to the Ebadi Institute—a ten-story social science building where the professor had his office—I saw what appeared to be some sort of student rally.

Tehran University had always been a bastion of political activity. In fact, the beginnings of the 1979 Iranian revolution had taken place at the entrance to the university.

Nevertheless, as soon as I got closer to the gathering, I realized the crowd assembled outside Ebadi Institute didn't have anything to do with a student protest. There were no speeches being made or chants going on, and, except for some low murmuring, it was eerily quiet for such a large group of people.

Suddenly, that silence was broken by the sound of an ambulance arriving. When I pushed my way up to the edge of the crowd, I understood why.

Splattered on the pavement in front of the Ebadi Institute was a dead body. From what I could tell, the person had either fallen or jumped from one of the floors in the building.

As soon as I looked up and spotted the broken window on the seventh floor, my stomach lurched. Professor Rouhani's office was on the seventh floor. It was located in the middle of a hallway containing five other offices.

Within seconds, I realized the victim had come from the middle window on the seventh floor, and I immediately began making my way over to where the ambulance had parked.

When I arrived, the ambulance attendants were moving the body onto a gurney. At first, I thought, the deceased couldn't possibly be Professor Rouhani since the professor was a very large man, and the mangled body I saw on the stretcher didn't look all that big.

However, that hope dissipated the instant the stretcher passed in front of me, and I recognized the lifeless body of Professor Bahram Rouhani.

I wasted no time leaving the area.

♦ ♦ ♦ ♦

I tried calling Aviz several times on my way over to the Vanak Recreational Center, but she never answered her phone. While I was tempted to call the facility itself and ask to speak to Aviz, I decided it wasn't the best time to draw attention to Hammid Salimi.

Calling the facility might not have made any difference, because by the time I pulled in the parking lot, there was an emergency vehicle in front of the building.

Seconds later, a military staff car pulled to the curb and General Lajani Davar, the father of Aviz, jumped out of the vehicle and rushed inside.

Shortly afterward, when several young women emerged from the building holding onto each other, I knew something terrible must have happened to Aviz.

When I saw one of the women approaching the vehicle next to mine, I got out of the Renault. "What's happening inside?" I asked. "Did someone get hurt?"

Tears were streaming down her face as she answered me. "Yes, it's one of my friends. She just . . . She's dead."

"Did she drown or—"

"No," she said, shaking her head. "She took a couple of drinks of her orange juice, and then she just collapsed on the floor."

"Was she—"

"I'm sorry," she said, opening her car door. "I can't talk about it."

After she pulled out of the parking lot, I got back inside the Renault and made an emergency call to Carlton.

Chapter 12

When Carlton ordered me back to the Avini apartment, he told me not to even think about driving by the bookstore where Fabel Reza worked.

Then, he gave me the bad news.

"The Ops Center just informed me Farid was taken to Evin Prison the moment he was arrested. For the past twenty-four hours, he's been subjected to intense interrogation, and, a couple of hours ago, he was given a fifteen-minute closed-door trial."

When he paused, I exploded. "Don't keep me in suspense, Douglas. Tell me what happened."

He cleared his throat. "They convicted him of espionage. He was sentenced to death by hanging."

"Farid's father will intervene. I'm sure of that."

"They've already carried out the sentence."

I couldn't speak.

"I'm sorry, Titus. I know this must be difficult for you."

I managed to croak out a couple of words. "I'm fine."

"We'll have to pull you out now."

"I get that."

"Stay at the safe house. Don't go anywhere or make contact with anyone while I make the arrangements."

I felt numb when I returned to the safe house. Just like that, in less than twenty-four hours, four of my assets had been murdered.

I imagined Reza had also been killed. That only left Omid Askari, who, as far as I knew, was still visiting relatives on the Caspian coast.

Was there any way I could save Omid? Was he even alive?

I knew it wouldn't take long for VEVAK to find out where Omid was vacationing; perhaps even now they were arresting him, along with the rest of his family.

I removed my computer from my carryall so I could look up the location of the town where Omid had taken his family. However, as soon as I opened up my laptop, I received a notification an email was waiting for me in my inbox.

It was from Omid.

"I got your text." he said. *"There's no cell phone service here in Chalus right now, but I'll be back in Tehran this evening, and I'll call you then."*

The message had been sent less than five hours ago.

Did VEVAK know Omid was on his way back to Tehran? Had they already dispatched agents to his house?

It didn't matter.

I left the Avini apartment and headed over there.

◆ ◆ ◆ ◆

Omid lived in a three-story residence on Karaneh Street in the Elahyieh district of northern Tehran, not far from Chaman's apartment. By the time I arrived, the streetlights had come on.

As I drove down the street, I was relieved to see Omid's house was completely dark. Although I was glad he wasn't home yet, my heart rate went up the moment I spotted a vehicle parked outside a residence at the end of the block.

When I drove by and saw it wasn't occupied, I immediately turned around, drove back down the street, and pulled to the curb opposite Omid's house.

Not surprisingly, my Agency sat phone began vibrating as soon as I turned off the car's engine. I felt certain the Ops Center had notified my handler I'd disobeyed his orders and left the safe house.

My pulsating blue dot on The Grid had given me away.

"What do you think you're doing?" Carlton asked.

"I got an email from Omid. He's on his way back to the city."

"When was it sent?"

"About six hours ago."

"No sign of VEVAK in the area?"

"None."

"Hold on. Let me pull up a map of the neighborhood."

While I was waiting for Carlton, I observed a vehicle making a right-hand turn onto Karaneh Street. I quickly slumped down in the front seat of the Renault until the headlights of the oncoming car had moved past me. Then, Carlton came back on the line again.

"Are you aware there's an alley in the back of Omid's house?" he asked.

"No, I haven't had a chance to do any recon yet."

"Stay put while I see what kind of satellite surveillance is available in that area."

"I'd prefer a drone if you have it."

"Your actions hardly merit preferential treatment."

◆ ◆ ◆ ◆

I didn't get a drone, but Carlton was able to get access to the feed from a reconnaissance satellite. Those images didn't show any activity in the alleyway behind Omid's residence.

After observing the house for a couple of hours, I decided it was time to go take a look inside. When I called Carlton, he didn't disagree with me.

"If Omid returns tonight, you must convince him to go with you to the safe house," he said. "Just because VEVAK hasn't shown up yet, doesn't mean they won't eventually. It may take them a few days to run down all the intel Farid has given them."

"What do you think triggered VEVAK's interest in Farid in the first place?"

"We'll explore that when you get back to Langley."

"It had to be Amir Madani."

"Our analysts have initiated a full spectrum data probe on him. If they missed something, the data mining will find it."

"Maybe I missed something."

"Right now, you need to concentrate on getting back to the safe house. Give Omid two more hours, and then leave the area immediately."

Carlton hung up after I assured him I had no plans to stick around the neighborhood any longer than necessary.

◆ ◆ ◆ ◆

It wasn't the first time I'd been in Omid's house when no one was home. Before recruiting him—when I'd needed to make sure he was exactly who he said he was—I'd explored every nook and cranny of the place.

Now, I entered Omid's house the same way—by picking the lock on the back door.

The house smelled musty, like it had been closed up for several days. While I considered the stuffy odor a promising sign a couple of VEVAK agents weren't waiting for me around the next corner, I still cleared every room.

Then, I sat down in the living area and waited for Omid to show up. As I sat there in the dark, I tried not to think about my dead assets.

That proved impossible.

Even though I'd had assets die before, this time it felt different.

Was it because I'd been careless? Had I been careless?

Was it because of the way my assets had died or was it simply death itself?

Death had always bothered me. It just seemed so senseless. Why come into existence at all if that existence was only temporary?

Was there life beyond death?

I doubted it.

However, if life beyond the grave did exist, then maybe death wouldn't seem so senseless. Maybe my life would have more meaning.

It was true. Beyond my duty to my country, my life didn't have much meaning, but—

Suddenly, I was startled out of my reverie when a set of headlights splashed across the front windows of the living room.

Someone had pulled into Omid's driveway.

When I took a quick peek through the windows, I immediately recognized Omid's car.

He was alone.

◆ ◆ ◆ ◆

I decided to wait in the living room before making my presence known to Omid. After the events of the day, I wasn't taking any chances.

After Omid came in the back door and turned on the lights in the kitchen, he opened up the refrigerator and took out a bottle of fruit juice. As he twisted the cap off, he strolled into the living room.

He appeared to be a man without a care in the world.

All that was about to change.

"Don't turn on the lights, Omid."

"Ahh!" he shouted, spilling fruit juice all over his shirt.

"It's only me," I said, coming out of the shadows.

"Hammid," he said with a deep sigh, "what are you doing here? How did you get in my house?"

His eyes suddenly fixated on the gun in my hand.

"I don't have time to explain everything right now, but you have to trust me. You're in danger, and you need to leave your house immediately. That's why I'm here. I want to take you to a place where you'll be safe."

"What? No, that's not possible. My family—"

"Where is your family?"

"They stayed a few extra days in Chalus. My uncle is very ill."

When he began telling me about his uncle's illness, he started talking very rapidly while pacing back and forth across the floor—signs he was experiencing an adrenaline rush.

I grabbed his arm. "Listen to me, Omid. Yesterday, VEVAK arrested a friend of mine. Like you, he's been feeding me information about the opposition. They immediately took him to Evin Prison." I paused a moment. "I'm sure you know what that means."

He looked terrified. "He's been tortured."

"That's right," I said calmly. "He's given them the names of all his contacts. Even though he didn't know about you, I was one of his contacts, so as soon as VEVAK starts putting together a list of all my acquaintances, you'll be on their radar."

"You and I have always been very careful."

I shook my head. "It won't matter. My cover story was excellent, but it wasn't infallible. They know who I am now, and they've already murdered four of my sources. I'm sure you're next on the list."

He flapped his hands nervously. "But you said VEVAK only arrested your friend yesterday."

"That's why we need to hurry. They're moving very quickly on this. Don't worry, though. I can get you out of Iran tonight. All you need to do is to come with me now."

"No," he said, shaking his head back and forth. "I can't leave my family behind."

I lied and said, "VEVAK won't hurt them, Omid. They never—"

His eyes suddenly lit up. "I'll go back to Chalus tonight. I can leave Iran from there. My family can go with me."

"There's no way you can—"

"No, Hammid, this will work. I promise you. Come with me; I'll show you."

Before I could stop him, Omid ran toward the stairs.

I took one last look out the window and followed him.

◆ ◆ ◆ ◆

Omid had a study on the third floor of his residence. It was filled with bookshelves, along with a comfortable chair and a large desk.

The room also contained a safe, and that's where Omid headed as soon as he entered the room. He was nervous, so it took him a couple of tries before he got the combination right and swung open the door.

Once the safe was opened, he began talking very rapidly in

disjointed sentences describing how he'd been preparing for this moment for years and telling me how he was planning to get his family out of Iran.

After he showed me the false passports he'd obtained for each member of his family, I finally agreed he should leave Tehran immediately and return to Chalus.

I helped him put the documents in a briefcase, along with a substantial amount of cash, and then we went down to the bedrooms on the second floor, where he selected one small item from each of the children's rooms. After stuffing these in the briefcase, we headed downstairs.

When we began descending the stairs to the first floor, Omid's disjointed chatter suddenly evolved into a stream of consciousness thing, and he seemed to be saying whatever came to his mind.

Mainly, he was talking about how he'd struggled as a young man to figure out what to do with his life, but then, once he had a family, everything fell into place.

Just before reaching the bottom of the staircase, he looked back at me and said, "Hammid, what's the most important thing in the world to you?"

At that moment, three VEVAK agents burst through the front door of Omid's house and shot him.

◆ ◆ ◆ ◆

As Omid tumbled down the stairs, I returned fire. I immediately knew I'd hit one of the agents dead center and wounded another one, but the third guy started up the stairs after me.

I turned and raced up to the third floor, where I knew the windows in Omid's study opened out onto the roof.

As I raised the window and climbed out on the flat roof, I heard the VEVAK agent enter the study behind me. He immediately fired his pistol at me, but his aim was off, and the bullet shattered the glass instead.

When I ran over to the other side of the roof—the side facing Omid's backyard—I expected to see VEVAK agents parked in the alley behind the house.

However, both the backyard and the alley were empty.

I estimated it was at least a thirty foot drop from the roof to the ground. Could I jump that distance and walk away?

I felt pretty sure I could, as long as I landed correctly.

I tried to remember the correct way to land in order to survive a jump from a three-story building.

Nothing immediately came to mind.

As the VEVAK agent came around the corner and aimed his pistol at me, I jumped anyway.

When I landed, everything went black.

PART THREE

Chapter 13

Tehran, Iran
January 7, 2015

I heard voices, but I couldn't figure out what they were saying. My mind felt fuzzy, like it was full of gauze, or cotton, or fluffy white clouds.

I floated on the clouds, soaring high, then dipping down to skim over the surface of a snow-capped mountain. The mountain resembled a man's face, and, seconds later, the man's features came into sharp focus.

"Mr. Qasim," I heard the man say, "can you hear me? Are you awake now?"

"I . . . What? . . ."

"You're in a hospital, Mr. Qasim. I'm Dr. Turani, and I'm taking you up to surgery now. You've been given something for your pain, so you should be feeling better soon."

I wanted to argue with the man who called himself a doctor. I wanted to tell him my name wasn't Qasim, and I didn't need any surgery. I felt perfectly fine. In fact, I felt better than fine; I felt wonderful.

As I struggled to explain my blissful state to the good doctor, another man's face floated into view.

It was Fabel Reza.

He bent down and whispered in my ear. "Don't worry, Hammid. Everything's going to be okay."

I wasn't worried.

Reza was the one who should be worried; Reza was dead.

Maybe I was dead too.

♦ ♦ ♦ ♦

The first person I saw when the fog finally lifted was Fabel Reza. He was seated in a chair beside my bed.

"Welcome back, my friend."

I tried to speak, but nothing came out.

Reza picked up a paper cup and offered me a sip of water. "Don't drink too fast; you might choke." After placing the plastic straw between my lips, he smiled and said, "Now, wouldn't that be ironic?"

Once I'd taken a few sips, I asked, "What happened? Where am I?"

"You're in Erfan Clinic. I'll explain what happened to you in a few minutes." He pulled a Syrian passport out of his shirt pocket and handed it to me. "You need to remember you're Sayid Qasim. You're a Syrian construction worker who fell off a building and shattered his leg. Dr. Turani and his team have just spent the last four hours putting it back together."

I suddenly became aware of a very large cast on my left leg.

"I broke my leg," I said, stating the obvious.

Reza laid his hand on the plaster cast and nodded. "You smashed your femur and tore all the ligaments in your knee."

"How did I get here?"

"My friends and I brought you."

"What friends?"

Reza pulled his chair closer to my bed and said, "I haven't been completely honest with you, Hammid." He shook his head. "I'm not talking about the information I've been giving you. I assure you that's been accurate. But, I've also been sharing that same information with my Israeli friends."

I couldn't tell if the drugs in my system were messing with my thought processes, so I asked him to repeat what he'd said.

He leaned in closer and whispered in my ear. "Besides working for you, I've also been working for Mossad."

Mossad, the Israeli intelligence agency, was notorious for double recruiting—running agents who worked for other intelligence services—so his revelation didn't come as a complete surprise to me.

"Is Mossad responsible for this?" I asked, holding up the Syrian passport he'd given me.

He nodded. "That's right. When my case officer informed me he was taking me to a safe house because VEVAK was looking for you, I told them I wouldn't go with them unless they helped me find you. I can't tell you how they were able to do that, but when they arrived at Omid Askari's residence, three agents from VEVAK had just entered the house.

"The Israelis decided it was safer for them to enter the house from the rear, so they drove their van around to the alley in the back of the house. We arrived just in time to see you jump from the roof, and when a VEVAK agent began firing at you a few seconds later, one of the Mossad agents shot him. After that, I helped them put you in their van, and we brought you over here to the clinic."

"I'm grateful for your help, Fabel. You saved my life."

"The danger's not over yet. Mossad is making arrangements to get you to a safe house, but the sooner we get you out of here, the better."

"Get my clothes," I said. "We can leave now."

As I was removing my hospital gown, Dr. Turani walked in the room. "What are you doing?" he asked.

I mumbled something about wanting to take a shower, but he shook his head and said a shower would have to wait.

When he rolled a blood pressure machine over to my bed, two other men entered the room; one was wearing a suit; the other one had on a tan sports jacket.

They didn't look like doctors.

◆ ◆ ◆ ◆

While Dr. Turani was taking my blood pressure, the two men stood by the door observing everything, but saying nothing.

"Very good," Dr. Turani said, removing the cuff from my arm.

Next, he used his stethoscope to listen to my heart. Finally, he stepped back and motioned toward the men. "He's able to travel now. Just make sure he stays hydrated."

The doctor looked over at Reza, who didn't appear the least bit concerned I was being handed over to the men. "Take good care of your friend," he said. "He needs lots of therapy."

Reza smiled and shook the doctor's hand. "I'll do that."

Dr. Turani turned and addressed me. "Mr. Qasim, if I may have your passport now, I'll get your discharge papers ready and then you'll be able to leave. The nurse should be here shortly with a wheelchair for you."

After I handed him the Syrian passport, he shook my hand and left the room. As soon as he was gone, the Tan Sports Jacket Guy walked over to my bed. The Suit Guy stayed where he was.

"Tell me your name," he demanded.

"Sayid Qasim."

"What happened to your leg?"

"I broke it when I fell off a building at a construction site."

"Which construction site was it?"

"Ah . . . Shahid Stadium. I was working on the new event center."

He looked pleased.

◆ ◆ ◆ ◆

Thirty minutes later, I was sitting in the backseat of a mini-van traveling down the Niayesh Expressway. In the seat next to me was the Tan Sports Jacket Guy who told me to call him Micha. His partner, who was driving the van, said his name was Ehud.

Like most Israeli operatives I'd known, their stoic faces made it nearly impossible for me to get a read on them. Both men were totally inscrutable.

If I had to guess, though, I'd say they weren't too happy they were putting their own lives in danger in order to rescue a CIA guy. Fabel Reza, on the other hand, seemed pleased he'd had a hand in saving my life.

Reza was in the front seat with Ehud, but he was facing toward the rear so he could hear what Micha was telling me.

Micha was telling me his superiors at the Office—a.k.a. Mossad—had gotten in touch with my superiors at the Agency—a.k.a. the DDO—and both parties had agreed I should remain in Tehran until my broken leg had healed.

From what I understood, Mossad was providing the safe house while the Agency was providing Mossad with the funds to run it.

"Once we drop you off at the safe house," Micha said, "you won't hear from us again. You'll be living with Javad Mirza and his family. His wife, Darya, is a nurse, and she'll be taking care of you while you recuperate. Once you're well enough to travel, Javad's uncle will make arrangements to get you out of Iran."

"Is VEVAK still looking for me?"

Micha nodded. "Our sources tell us VEVAK has issued a high priority alert for your arrest. They've identified you as an American spy who murdered two of their agents."

He reached inside his jacket and pulled out a cell phone. "I was told to give you this encrypted cell phone. One of your superiors should be contacting you shortly."

"Any idea what happened to my sat phone?"

"We destroyed it. We thought it might have been compromised."

I found that highly unlikely, but I was in no position to argue with him.

I was in no position to do anything.

◆ ◆ ◆ ◆

After Ehud turned off the Sangab Highway onto Kohestan Boulevard in western Tehran, I noticed he kept glancing in his rearview mirror, while making a series of lane changes.

I remembered the Kohestan district was largely a residential area, so I figured his evasive procedures probably indicated the safe house was nearby.

This was confirmed a few minutes later when he glanced back at

Micha and said, "We're clean."

After Micha replied, "Proceed," Ehud made a right-hand turn at the next intersection and entered a narrow residential street, where each of the modest looking homes was surrounded by a high concrete fence.

When Ehud slowed down about halfway down the block, a man standing to the side of a wrought iron gate immediately swung it open, and Ehud drove inside.

The short driveway led up to a single-story residence constructed of rough-hewn bricks and concrete. It was a nondescript structure, but it was to be my safe haven for the next few weeks.

"This is where we say goodbye," Micha said.

I shook his hand. "Thanks for your help. Perhaps I can return the favor someday."

He shrugged. "Maybe."

As I was telling Reza goodbye, the man who'd opened the gate for us, walked up to the van. After speaking with Micha for a few minutes, he went inside the house and came out a few seconds later carrying a pair of crutches.

When he walked over to the car and handed me the crutches, he smiled and said, "I'm Javad Mirza. Welcome to my home."

◆ ◆ ◆ ◆

Although I was pretty shaky, I managed to use the crutches to get from the van to the front door of the safe house. As soon as Javad opened the door, I heard Ehud put the van in reverse and start backing out of the driveway.

I glanced back over my shoulder in time to see the van pull into the street and disappear around the corner.

Suddenly, without warning, I experienced a torrent of emotions as I thought about how my life had changed in the last forty-eight hours.

I'd gone from living the life of a wealthy businessman in a luxurious apartment in Shemiran, where I'd had a closet full of clothes and a well-stocked refrigerator, to being on the run from the secret police and having to depend on a couple of strangers to take care of me. Although I'd been in tight spots before, I couldn't remember a time when I'd ever felt so alone and disoriented.

Whether it was the aftereffects of the drugs in my system or my emotional state, a few seconds later, I felt the room start to spin and the crutches slip from my grasp.

As I struggled to keep my balance, Javad immediately came to my rescue and helped me into a sagging recliner.

"Easy now," he said. "Are you okay?"

"It's the drugs."

"Of course. Let me get you some water."

Javad walked across the living room to a small kitchen and grabbed a bottle of water out of the refrigerator.

As he handed it to me, he said, "Do you want me to call you Hammid Salimi or Sayid Qasim?"

"Hammid Salimi," I said.

It was all I had left.

Chapter 14

Tehran, Iran
March 7, 2015

When I noticed the date on the front page of the *Al Alam,* one of Tehran's leading newspapers, I suddenly realized I'd been living at the safe house for two months.

Although I was surprised to see two months had gone by since the Israeli agents had delivered me to Javad's house, my shock at seeing the date wasn't because the days had flown by.

Quite the contrary.

Ever since I'd arrived at the safe house, my days had moved at a snail's pace; there had even been days when I'd asked myself if time had come to a complete stop altogether.

Before Operation Torchlight, I'd been on a few missions when I'd been required to spend several days at a safe house doing nothing. But, during those times, when I'd just been sitting around, I'd also been planning the next phase of the operation, going over possible scenarios, or figuring out an alternative escape route.

However, other than doing the physical exercises Darya had given me, my days at the safe house had been spent doing absolutely nothing, or, at least, nothing of significance.

Shortly after my arrival, when Javad had asked me what he could do to help me pass the time, I'd asked him to pick up a newspaper on his way home from work every day.

I'd specifically asked him for the *Al Alam* newspaper because, not only did it contain the most up-to-date news about the hardliners in the Iranian regime, it also contained a daily crossword puzzle.

For the past two months, that's how I'd been spending my days—doing crossword puzzles, which was amazing in itself, because I'd never been a big fan of crossword puzzles. In reality, I'd always considered them a complete waste of time.

I still did.

However, I knew the discipline and cognition required to work a crossword puzzle in Farsi was good for me, and the process also took up a few hours of my time each day.

In addition to working crossword puzzles every day, I'd also been spending my time studying moves on a chessboard.

One evening, not long after my arrival, Javad had suggested we get a game of chess going, and I'd immediately agreed, even though I hadn't played the game since my college days.

Little did I know, Javad was an excellent chess player.

When we'd first started playing, he'd won every game. Gradually, though, after studying his plays, I'd learned to anticipate his moves and make my moves accordingly.

Strangely enough, when I'd won my first game, Javad had expressed more excitement about my victory than I had, and he'd even called Darya into the living room to tell her the news.

Although Darya didn't play chess herself, she'd reacted with enthusiasm and congratulated me.

Their response to my victory was typical of how the two of them related to me. No matter what I attempted to do—whether it was taking my first steps when my cast was removed, or cooking an Iranian pastry—they were always encouraging me.

I'd never met anyone like them.

◆ ◆ ◆ ◆

From our very first meeting, I could tell there was something different about Javad and his family.

At first, I couldn't put my finger on what it was, but, after we'd been together for a few days, I was sure I'd figured it out; it was their attitude, specifically their optimism—they seemed much less cynical than most Iranians and far more hopeful.

But, when I'd commented on it to Javad, he'd immediately attributed their positive attitude to their faith.

He told me they were followers of Jesus Christ.

I was shocked by this revelation.

Here I was, an American spy, wanted by the secret police, and I was being sheltered in the home of some Iranian Christians, who were themselves under police scrutiny.

The first chance I got, I brought this up with Carlton.

◆ ◆ ◆ ◆

Three days after I arrived at the safe house, I received a call from Carlton on the phone Micha had given me. I could tell he was anxious about something the moment I heard his voice.

"I'll keep this short," he said. "I know you'll understand why."

I had no clue.

"Sure," I said. "I completely understand."

After talking with him for a few minutes, I realized he was probably anxious about the phone itself—he'd always been skittish of any communication device not issued by the Agency.

When I thought the conversation was drawing to a close, I asked him if he knew the Iranians in charge of the safe house were Christians. He assured me he did, and he said it was nothing I should worry about.

When I heard that, all my pent-up emotions burst forth in one long angry rant. My tirade was full of disparaging remarks about how the Agency hadn't protected my assets, and I also threw in a few paragraphs describing how I felt about being confined to a safe house for several months.

When I finally ended my tantrum, instead of Carlton chiding me about my anger issues—which he often did whenever I lost my temper—all he said was, "I'll call you next week."

After that, he disconnected the call.

Later, I told myself if Carlton wasn't concerned about Mossad placing me in a safe house run by Iranian Christians, then I shouldn't be either.

Of course, Carlton wasn't living with the Christians; I was.

♦ ♦ ♦ ♦

Christianity wasn't something I'd given much thought to until I was forced to live with Javad and Darya. Perhaps I'd ignored it because I hadn't been brought up in a religious home; no one in my family had ever shown any interest in God, the Bible, or attending a church service.

In reality, because I'd had to pose as an ardent Islamist on several occasions, I'd probably given more thought to the teachings of Mohammed, than I'd ever given to the teachings of Christ.

All that changed shortly after I arrived at the safe house.

Once Javad told me he and his family were Christians, they were very open about discussing their faith with me, and they didn't try to hide their religious practices, especially their habit of reading the Bible together, which they did every night following the evening meal.

After the meal, as Darya began removing the dishes from the table, I'd retreat over to my bed in a corner of their tiny living room, while Javad, Darya, and Mansoor remained at the kitchen table.

Javad would always begin by saying a prayer, then each of them would read aloud from a small, well-worn Bible. Afterward, they would discuss what they'd read.

Although I tried to occupy myself by reading the newspaper or working a crossword puzzle, I couldn't help but hear the Scriptures they were reading and what they were saying.

As soon as they were finished, Javad would return the Bible to its hiding place behind a wall in their living room.

Even though they knew anyone professing Christianity in Iran faced intense persecution, including torture, imprisonment, and murder, they didn't seem to be intimidated by this prospect when I brought it up.

Javad assured me he was aware of the risks they were taking, but he said each member of his family was ready to give their lives for Christ even as Christ had given his life for them. While I was astonished by his response and in awe of their courage, what I found incomprehensible was the joy each of them exhibited in these circumstances.

To my complete surprise, as I listened to their discussions every night, I began to question whether the dull ache I sometimes felt in my own life could be the result of my lack of faith in God.

After a few weeks had gone by, I got up the courage to share my feelings with Javad.

"These are good questions you're asking, Hammid."

"I didn't know I was asking a question."

"Oh, but you are," he said, pointing his finger at my heart. "You're asking questions in here, and that's where faith first begins. When your dead heart comes alive, that's a gift from God. He's showing you mercy, showering you with his grace, even though you've done nothing to deserve it."

"I don't think that's true, Javad. I've always been a good—"

"Here, let me show you what I mean."

Javad walked over and removed the Bible from its hiding place. When he opened it up, he pointed to a verse of Scripture and insisted I read it aloud to him.

Although I'd read the Quran several times, the words from the Quran never affected me the way the words from the Bible did.

The more I talked with Javad, the more I realized I wanted to have what he had. He described it as "a relationship with the Lord."

I had no clue what that meant.

But, I thought about it all the time.

Chapter 15

Tehran, Iran
April 1, 2015

As Rahim Mirza briefed me on the final details of Mossad's plan to get me out of Iran and back to the States, I felt a sense of excitement I hadn't felt since I'd stood on the roof of Omid's house and calculated how far down it was.

It was like I was back in the game.

Rahim, who was Javad's uncle, identified himself as a Courier, the title Mossad used for someone responsible for smuggling people and parcels out of a hostile country.

The most important quality a Courier possessed was confidence, and when Rahim was explaining the two-day trip we were about to make from Tehran to the Iranian/Turkey border crossing at Bazargan, Iran, he expressed little doubt he would be able to deliver me into the hands of the CIA's station chief in Turkey.

"I've made this trip many times before, and I've never had a problem," he said. "I'm not saying the journey will be easy, especially with that leg of yours, but I assure you it will be successful."

Rahim had the perfect cover for a Courier. He was a farmer who grew apples for a living, and for years now, he'd been making monthly deliveries of his produce to a market in Dogubayazit, Turkey.

When he pulled a crumpled map out of his pocket and traced the route we would take from Tehran into northern Iran and on to

Turkey, he assured me the border guards at the Bazargan crossing knew him well. "Sometimes, they even wave me through the crossing without ever inspecting my vehicle," he said.

"Are you sure I can fit in the trunk of your car?" I asked.

He nodded. "I've transported much larger men than you."

Darya spoke up, "Rahim, you must stop every few hours and let Hammid get out of the trunk so he can exercise his leg. Otherwise, he won't be able to walk when he gets there."

"I'll do my best."

Javad pointed over to the black cane beside my chair, "Don't forget your cane, Hammid. I'm sure you'll need it."

I didn't know whether to be angry or amused at the way Javad and Darya were treating me, but I could hardly blame them for sounding so patronizing when they'd only seen me as an invalid for the past three months, someone who sat around all day playing chess or working crossword puzzles.

I felt certain they couldn't imagine I'd been responsible for planning much larger and more dangerous operations than the one Rahim was planning.

"That's it then," Rahim said, folding up his map. "We'll leave at dawn tomorrow."

"Don't worry," I said. "I'll be ready when you get here."

As we got up from the kitchen table, Javad walked over and stood between Rahim and me. Placing his hand on each of our shoulders, he said, "Allow me to say a prayer for your safety."

"Yes," Darya said, calling for Mansoor to come and join us, "we must pray for you before you go."

Before I knew what was happening, everyone had joined hands—me included.

As we stood there, shoulder to shoulder, Javad made an impassioned plea for God's hand to deliver Rahim and me through the mountains of Iran and into Turkey without incident. He ended his prayer by asking God to grant me a special blessing as I returned home to America.

It was a beautiful, fervent prayer. One I would never forget.

◆ ◆ ◆ ◆

I was too wired to go to bed after Rahim had left; so once everyone else had gone to bed, I sat down in Javad's recliner and started working on my last crossword puzzle.

It wasn't long before I realized I was having trouble concentrating. All I could think about was leaving Tehran tomorrow.

I didn't believe I'd ever return, and I kept asking myself if the two years I'd spent here in Tehran, and the intel I'd gathered, had been worth the lives of the assets I'd lost.

I was also haunted by Chaman's face the last time I'd seen her in Jamshidieh Park in front of the statue of Abolqasem Ferdowsi. What had happened to her? Had she also been arrested?

I felt certain she knew nothing of Farid's activities, but that would hardly matter to VEVAK.

As I thought about the way I'd treated her—using her to further my own agenda with Amir Madani, not to mention failing to warn her the secret police might be coming after her—I began to feel guilty in a way I'd never felt before.

When I tried to rationalize my actions as necessary to carrying out my mission, I suddenly became aware of other instances when I'd been heartless or even cruel toward those who were peripheral to an operation.

I had always considered myself a pretty good person, but now, for the first time in my life, I began to question whether that was true or not.

After Javad had shown me a verse in the Bible that said everyone had sinned, he'd explained I would need to recognize myself as a sinner before I could ever have a relationship with the Lord. He'd told me that was the first step.

Had I just taken that first step?

◆ ◆ ◆ ◆

Although I was sure I couldn't sleep, I crawled into bed anyway, but, just before I turned off the lamp, Javad walked in the room.

When he came over and knelt down beside me, he also appeared to be wide awake. "Hammid," he said, putting his hand on my arm, "before you leave, I must ask you a very important question."

"Okay, Javad, ask me your question."

"Will you make a commitment to become a follower of Jesus Christ?"

"Yes, Javad, I will."

He didn't seem surprised.

The next day, when Rahim and I left for Turkey, I felt my life had just begun.

I wasn't wrong.

A NOTE TO MY READERS

Dear Reader, Thank you for reading *One Step Back,* the prequel to *One Night in Tehran,* Book I in the Titus Ray Thriller Series. If you enjoyed this novella, you'll enjoy reading my full-length novels in the series. Purchase links are available at LuanaEhrlich.com.

Would you consider signing up for my newsletter? It's a monthly publication that contains insider information about Titus Ray, plus updates about the books in this series. When you sign up, I'll send you a FREE COPY of *Titus Ray Thriller Recipes and Short Stories* for your Kindle device.

You can sign up for my newsletter at LuanaEhrlich.com and find out more about me and Titus Ray Thrillers at TitusRayThrillers.com.

One of my greatest blessings comes from receiving email from my readers. My email address is author@luanaehrlich.com. I'd love to hear from you!

Here's an added bonus: On the following pages are the opening chapters to *One Night in Tehran,* Book I in the Titus Ray Thriller Series. Enjoy!

ONE NIGHT IN TEHRAN
Prologue

In far northwest Iran, a few minutes after clearing the city limits of Tabriz, Rahim maneuvered his vehicle onto a rutted side road. When he popped opened the trunk of the car to let me out, I saw the car was hidden from the main highway by a small grove of trees. In spite of our seclusion, Rahim said he was still anxious about being seen by a military convoy from the nearby Tabriz missile base.

For the first time in several hours, I uncurled from my fetal position and climbed out of the vehicle, grateful to breathe some fresh air and feel the sunshine on my face. As my feet landed on the rocky terrain, Rahim handed me a black wooden cane. I wanted to wave it off, but, regrettably, I still needed some help getting around on my bum leg.

Rahim slammed the trunk lid down hard.

"You can stretch for a few minutes," he said, "but then we must get back on the road immediately. Our timing must be perfect at the border."

Rahim and I were headed for the Iranian/Turkish border, specifically the border crossing at Bazargan, Iran. He was absolutely confident he could get me out of Iran without any problems. However, during the last twenty years, I'd had a couple of incidents at other border crossings—Pakistan and Syria to be precise—so I wasn't as optimistic.

While Rahim was tinkering with the car's engine, I exercised my legs and worked out the stiffness in my arms. As usual, I was running through several "what ifs" in my mind. What if the border guards searched the trunk? What if the car broke down? What if we were driving right into a trap?

I might have felt better about any of these scenarios had either of us been armed. However, Rahim had refused to bring along a weapon. Carrying a gun in Iran without a special permit meant certain imprisonment. Imprisonment in Iran meant certain torture, so I *certainly* understood his reasons for leaving the weaponry back in Tehran.

Still, a gun might have helped my nerves.

I was surprised to hear Rahim say I could ride in the front passenger seat for the next hour. He explained the road ahead was usually deserted, except for a farm truck or two, so it seemed the perfect time to give me a brief respite from my cramped quarters.

I didn't argue with him.

However, I thought Rahim was being overly cautious having me ride in the trunk in the first place—at least until we got nearer the Turkish border. I'd been passing myself off as an Iranian of mixed ancestry back in Tehran, and now, having grown out my beard, I didn't believe a passing motorist would give me a second look.

When I climbed in the front seat, the cloying smell of ripe apples emanating from the back seat of Rahim's vehicle was especially pungent. Flat boxes of golden apples were piled almost as high as the back window, and the sweet-smelling fruit permeated the stuffy interior of the car. On the floorboard, there were several packages wrapped in colorful wedding paper. I was sure they reeked of ripe apples.

We had been back on the road for about twenty minutes when Rahim said, "Hand me one of those apples and take one for yourself, Hammid."

Although Rahim knew my true identity, he continued to address me by the name on my Swiss passport, Hammid Salimi, the passport I'd used to enter Iran two years ago. Unfortunately, it was now a name quite familiar to VEVAK, the Iranian secret police, who had already prepared a cell for me at Evin Prison in northwest Tehran.

After we had both devoured the apples, Rahim rolled down his window and threw the cores down a steep embankment.

"When you get back inside the trunk," he said, "you'll have to share your space with some of those." He gestured toward the apple boxes in the backseat.

I glanced over at him to see if he was joking, but, as usual, his brown, weather-beaten face remained impassive. Although I'd spent the last three months living with Rahim's nephew, Javad, and learning to discern Javad's emotional temperature simply by the set of his mouth or the squint of his eyes, I'd barely spent any time with Rahim. During the last two days together, he'd never made any attempt at humor, and it didn't appear he was about to start now.

I protested. "There's barely enough room for me back there."

"It will be snug with the boxes, but you will fit," he said. "If the guards open the trunk, I want them to see apples."

I felt a sudden flash of anger. "Before we left Tehran, you told me they wouldn't open the trunk at the border. You said they wouldn't even search the car."

My voice sounded harsh and loud in the small confines of the car.

However, Rahim calmly replied, "They will not search the car, Hammid. They have never searched inside. They have never searched the trunk. It is only a precaution."

He turned and looked directly at me, his penetrating black eyes willing me to trust him. It was a look I instantly recognized. I had used that same look on any number of assets, urging them to ferret out some significant nugget of intel and pass it on to me, even though I knew the odds of their being caught were high.

He returned his eyes to the road. "Surely you're acquainted with making minor changes as a plan evolves."

I took a deep breath. "You're right, of course." I suddenly felt foolish at my amateur reaction. "Planning for the unexpected is always smart. The more precautions you want to take, the better it will be for both of us. I'm sorry for questioning you."

For the first time, I saw a brief smile on his face. "There's no need to apologize," he said quietly. "The last three months have been difficult for you. Your paranoia is understandable."

Rahim shifted into a lower gear as we approached a steep incline. When we finally rounded a curve on the mountainous road, our attention was immediately drawn to two military vehicles parked on the opposite side of the road about one-half mile ahead of us. Several men were standing beside two trucks. They were smoking cigarettes and looking bored.

"It's not a roadblock," I said.

"No, we're fine."

Suddenly a man in uniform, leaning against the front bumper of the lead truck, noticed our approach and quickly took a couple of steps onto the highway. He signaled for us to pull over.

"Say nothing unless they speak to you first," Rahim said. "My papers are inside the glove box. Do not open it unless I say, 'Show them our papers.'"

"I have no papers, Rahim."

He eased the car onto the side of the road. "I put them inside the glove box," he said, "but don't open it unless I tell you to do so."

As the military officer crossed over the highway toward our car, I watched the reaction of the men standing outside the two vehicles. Although the insignia on the officer's uniform indicated he was a captain in the Iranian Revolutionary Guard Corps (IRGC), the men traveling with him were not in uniform. However, that didn't mean they weren't soldiers.

In fact, as I studied them, I knew they had to be affiliated with some aspect of Iran's vast military organization. They wore nearly identical Western clothing, had short military haircuts, and all their beards were regulation trim.

No longer bored, the men appeared alert now as their captain approached our car.

To my surprise, Rahim was opening the door and getting out of the car before the captain spoke one word to him. His behavior went against one of my favorite tenets of tradecraft: never draw attention to yourself.

The soft-spoken man I had been traveling with for two days suddenly disappeared. Instead, a loud, fast-talking stranger took his place.

"Captain," Rahim asked, "how may I assist you today? Did you have a breakdown? What a lonely stretch of road on which to be stranded."

Within seconds of greeting the captain, Rahim threw his arm around his shoulders and walked him away from our car and back across the road. There, Rahim engaged in conversation with some of the men, and, at one point, they all broke into laughter at something he said.

After a minute or two, I saw the captain draw Rahim away from the group and speak to him privately. Although I could hear none of their conversation, I tensed up when the captain gestured across the highway toward me. As Rahim continued an animated conversation with him, they began walking back across the road together.

Arriving at the car, Rahim opened the back door and pulled out two boxes of the apples we were transporting.

"Here you are, Captain. Take two of these. I'll bring two more for your men. You will not find finer apples in all of Iran."

As the captain leaned down to take the apples from Rahim, he glanced inside the interior of the car, quickly taking note of the apples, the wedding presents, and the black cane I'd placed between my legs. Lastly, his scrutiny fell on my face.

I smiled and deferentially lowered my head toward him, greeting him in Farsi. He didn't respond, but Rahim was speaking to him at the same time, so I wasn't sure he'd heard me.

The captain was already walking back to the transport trucks when Rahim stuck his head back inside the car and removed two other boxes.

Our eyes met.

He nodded at me. I nodded back.

Everything was fine.

While Rahim was distributing the apples among the men, I took the opportunity to look inside the glove box. I found three items: Rahim's passport, his travel documentation, and a small handgun.

Presumably, the handgun was my documentation had the captain demanded it.

There was something about having a fighting chance that did

wonders for my morale, and I found myself smiling.

I shut the glove box before Rahim returned.

I decided not to say anything to him about my discovery.

Without a word, Rahim got back inside the car and started the engine. As we drove past the captain and his men, several of them raised their apples to us in a goodbye salute.

"That was quite a performance, Rahim."

He continued to glance at his rear-view mirror until the group disappeared from sight.

Finally, he said, "The captain only wanted information on road conditions. He said he'd heard there were some rockslides in the area. One of the drivers was complaining about his brakes, and he was worried about the safety of his men as they made the descent."

"Who were those men? What unit did they belong to?"

"The captain didn't say, but their cigarettes came from Azerbaijan. That should tell you something."

Azerbaijan bordered Iran and was about six hours north of our location. Although it had once been a part of the Soviet Union, it was now an independent republic with close ties to Iran. Like most Iranians, the majority of the people were Shia Muslims. Tehran wanted to keep it that way. I'd heard rumors there was a unit of Iran's military specifically assigned to make sure the Sunni minority in Azerbaijan remained the minority. The unit in charge of such an operation was the *al Quds* force.

"Members of *al Quds*, then?"

"That's my guess. We've been hearing reports the Sunnis are growing in popularity. Tehran won't sit still while that happens. But that's good. Mossad likes it when Tehran is distracted."

"Why wasn't the captain interested in me?"

"I told him you were my father, plus you look harmless, Hammid."

It was true. I'd lost weight during my three-month ordeal, and, since I'd spent the time indoors, my skin had taken on an unhealthy pallor. However, I doubted I looked old enough to be his father.

"I also told him you'd fallen in the orchard and injured your leg. He wasn't surprised at your reluctance to get out of the car, if that's what you're thinking."

I remembered the way the captain had inspected the contents of our car and his lingering look at my cane. He may have believed Rahim, but he had checked out his story anyway.

"You said you were on your way to your cousin's wedding in Dogubayazit?"

"Yes, and if I hadn't given him the apples, he might have inquired further about the gifts." He flicked his hand toward the wedding presents on the backseat floorboard. "Then, I would have insisted he take one or two of those gifts for his sister."

As in most Middle Eastern countries, bribes and "gifts" were a way of life among the people, especially with military and government officials. Nothing got done without them. If you made inquiries or requested help from any bureaucrat, they expected something in return.

"You were very generous with the apples back there. Will you have enough for your friends at the border now?"

I tried not to sound worried, but whenever I found myself involved in someone else's operation, I got nervous.

He was dismissive. "Yes, there will be plenty. Now help me find the turnoff road. It leads over to a lake, but the sign is hard to see. We'll make the switch there."

He slowed down, and we both concentrated on the passing landscape. The trees were dense, and the late afternoon shadows made finding the lake road difficult.

"I think it's coming up," Rahim said.

I pointed off to my right. "There it is."

He made a sharp right turn onto a dirt road leading through a canopy of trees. One-half mile down the road, a secondary road branched off, and Rahim was able to make a U-turn at the fork in the road. Then, he pointed the car back toward the main highway.

Rahim killed the engine, and, after glancing down at his watch, he looked over at me. At that point, I knew I was about to be given The Speech, a last-minute review an operations officer usually gave to a subordinate before a critical phase commenced.

Technically, I wasn't a subordinate of Rahim's organization.

Still, I listened carefully.

"Remember the traffic at the border will move very slowly, and, once I'm pulled over, I expect there will be a long wait. At times, you will hear loud voices. That's not a cause for worry. If you hear angry voices, especially my angry voice, you should start to worry."

He paused for a long moment. Then, he opened the glove box and removed the handgun I'd seen earlier.

He handed it over to me with an understanding smile. "I'm assuming you found this already."

I checked the chamber.

It was loaded.

"Thanks, Rahim."

"Any questions?"

"No. I'm confident you've thought of everything."

We both got out of the car, and I helped him remove some of the apple boxes so he could stack them in the trunk after I was inside.

Before climbing in, I said, "Rahim, please hear me when I say I'm grateful for everything you and Javad have done for me. Perhaps, someday, I can repay you."

Rahim placed his hands on my shoulders and looked into my eyes. "That will never be necessary, Hammid," he said. "It has been God's will for us to help you."

As I tucked myself into the trunk again, I found myself hoping it was also God's will for me to make it out of Iran alive.

Chapter 1

Bill Lerner looked like a worried grandfather when he patted me on my knee in the backseat of the Lincoln Town Car and asked, "What's your state of mind, son?"

Our driver, Jamerson, gave me a quick glance in the rearview mirror.

I knew Jamerson had probably heard Lerner ask other intelligence officers that same question whenever he escorted them from Andrews AFB to one of the Agency safe houses in the quiet residential neighborhoods around McLean, Virginia.

I could hear the uncertainty in my voice as I responded, "I'm not sure, Bill, but it's good to be home."

Lerner ran his hand over his military-style haircut and shot back enthusiastically. "You bet. We'll get you debriefed, fix you up with some good grub, and then you'll be ready for some R & R."

Lerner's conversations never varied much.

His job consisted of making sure I felt safe—both he and the driver were armed—providing a listening ear if I needed to talk, and being the first in a long line of people who would bring me, a Level 1 covert operative, back to some sense of normalcy.

Lerner gestured toward my left leg, which I'd been massaging as we drove along. "That giving you trouble?"

"Yeah, a bit."

Once again, Jamerson stole a glance at me in the mirror. What was up with this guy? Was it just curiosity or something else?

I tried to dismiss my paranoia as nerves, pure and simple.

For the past several months, I'd been living on the edge in Tehran. However, three days ago, with Rahim's help, I'd made my escape from Iran, crossing the border into Turkey without incident.

Nevertheless, because I couldn't just turn my instincts on and off like a water spigot, I continued to mull over Jamerson's interest in me.

Lerner pointed to a large house at the top of a winding lane. "Well, in these new digs" he said, "you'll have some state-of-the-art rehab equipment for that leg. Support purchased this little *casa* for a song during the housing bust." He laughed. "It's been remodeled to our specifications, of course."

I didn't laugh.

I was too numb.

We pulled in front of the *"casa,"* which was at least a 10,000 square-foot house. It was surrounded by gigantic oak trees, and, in the distance, at the back of the house, I spotted a large lake with a boat dock. As we pulled into the circle drive, I half expected to see a butler and several uniformed maids appear at the front door to welcome the master of the castle home.

The house was well situated on several acres of forested land and located within a gated neighborhood of similar residences. I imagined most of the well-to-do owners had their own security systems. We had entered the safe house property through a remote-controlled sliding gate, and I suspected security cameras had been tracking us ever since.

"This one is called The Gray," Lerner said.

The name made sense. Instead of addresses or numbers, the Agency used color-coded names for their safe houses, and, while the exterior of the house was blindingly white, the window shutters and the front door were painted a muted shade of bluish gray.

Previously, I had been debriefed in The Red. It was at least half the size of this one and had a red-tiled roof. There was no butler, just a slightly plump Italian cook named Angelina who had helped me gain back the weight I'd lost on a mission into Pakistan. The neighbors thought I was her son. The complexion I'd inherited from my father made it easy for me to pass myself off as an Italian, or even an Iranian of mixed ancestry.

Lerner got out of the car and headed for the front door. "Jamerson, get his kit from the trunk and meet us inside."

I took my time getting out of the car.

I paused to zip up the jacket of the tracksuit I'd been issued at the air base in Turkey, and then I leaned back inside the car and picked up the cane from the back seat. All the while, I was keeping an eye on Jamerson. He grabbed the duffel bag given to me on the flight over from Turkey, and, when he closed the trunk, our eyes met.

He motioned toward the front entrance with a slight nod of his head. "After you, sir."

I was almost six feet tall, and he was about my height, but, unlike me, he had a beefy body. I wondered how many hours he spent in the gym each day.

I hadn't seen the inside of a gym for years.

I hobbled toward the door, thankful Jamerson hadn't offered to help me.

In fact, if he had, I might have marshaled whatever strength I had left and slugged him.

Pride was a great energizer for me.

Lerner was already standing inside the giant foyer of the mansion, having keyed in the front door's security code beyond the range of my prying eyes. He was speaking in hushed tones to a middle-aged couple. I presumed they were the homeowners—at least to the other residents in the neighborhood.

After Jamerson had deposited my duffel bag on the floor, I asked him, "Ex-Marine?"

"Yes, sir."

"You served at the American Embassy in Iraq in 2008?"

There was no mistaking the pride in his voice. "Yes, sir. I'm surprised you even remembered me. You weren't in very good shape that day."

"How could I forget—?"

"Greg and Martha," Lerner said, interrupting our conversation, "let me introduce you to your newest houseguest."

As Lerner steered them in my direction, Jamerson gave me an understanding nod, and I turned my attention to the couple in charge of the safe house.

Greg was in his late fifties with a slight paunch around his middle and close-cropped gray hair. He smiled at me with a lop-sided grin. His wife was petite, had short black hair and piercing blue eyes.

I shook their outstretched hands.

"Titus Ray," I said.

Martha's smile was warm. "Welcome home, Titus."

◆ ◆ ◆ ◆

Martha immediately took me on a "tour" of the house. It lasted almost thirty minutes. On the first floor, besides the huge eat-in kitchen, dining room, living room, and den, there was also a study, a library, and a media room.

I was sure the basement level was like no other house in the area. Three rooms made up a mini-hospital with an operating table, x-ray apparatus, laboratory facilities, and a pharmacy. There were also fully equipped physical therapy rooms and a soundproof conference room, wired with state-of-the-art audio and video equipment.

Upstairs, along with the master suite occupied by Greg and Martha, there were six bedrooms. Security officers were in two of the bedrooms, but I was the only guest of The Gray at the moment.

As Martha escorted me to my room, she casually mentioned other facilities, so I suspected there had to be a safe room somewhere, plus a room for all the security and communications equipment. Those rooms were either located on the basement level, or in a part of the house I would have to discover for myself.

My bedroom was at the end of the upstairs hallway, the furthest from the master suite and next door to one of the security officers' rooms. As soon as Martha left me alone, I opened the wooden shutters and spent a few minutes appreciating the view.

The manicured landscape included a large boulder waterfall with a cobblestone path running alongside it. I assumed the path led down to the lake. I suspected there might even be a tunnel from the basement right down to the dock and boathouse. Most safe houses remodeled by Support had secret exits somewhere.

Within an hour of my arrival, Greg appeared at my bedroom door. He informed me I was scheduled to see Dr. Terry Howard in the basement "hospital" for a physical.

It would not be my first encounter with Terry Howard.

Howard and I had met when I was recruited by the CIA in 1980 in the middle of the Iran hostage crisis. My time at The Farm, the CIA's training facility at Camp Peary in Williamsburg, Virginia, had been full of surprises, one of which had been a case of appendicitis.

About two hours into a three-day training exercise, I had noticed a slight pain in my right side. Howard, who had just completed his residency at Massachusetts General Hospital in emergency medicine, was a member of our four-person squad, and when I popped a couple of aspirin, he started to suspect something was wrong with me. However, our team had come in last in our previous exercise, and, as the team leader, I was determined it wasn't going to happen again, so I kept ignoring my discomfort.

The task took place in and around Raleigh, North Carolina and involved locating a human target, eliminating the hostiles—another squad of trainees—and delivering the target across a "border." The border in this case was the Virginia state line.

By midnight of the first night, as my team and I were meeting together in a cheap motel on the outskirts of Raleigh, I started vomiting. After one such trip to the bathroom, Howard ignored my feeble objections and pushed on my belly. He ended his exam by asking me some ridiculous questions. Finally, he announced I was having an appendicitis attack and wanted me to check into a hospital.

I angrily disagreed and insisted on completing the task first, so Howard backed off for a couple of hours. However, after the four of us determined the location of our target, my pain became noticeably more intense.

At that point, Howard started hammering me with the facts of a burst appendix.

His lecture convinced me to work out a compromise with him.

Without informing anyone at The Farm, Howard took me to the ER at Duke Raleigh Hospital and made arrangements with a surgeon to remove my diseased organ. From my hospital bed the next day, I continued to direct our mission, using one of the team members as my messenger. On the third day, our target was secured, so the team picked me up from the hospital, and we made our run for the border.

Unfortunately, we came in second.

However, none of our trainers ever found out about my emergency appendectomy. The only time they questioned me was before my initial overseas assignment. Then, the examining physician noticed my scar and remarked that someone had failed to enter my appendectomy on my medical records. At that point, I backdated the operation's date, and that was the end of it.

After our training, Dr. Terry Howard had been assigned to the Middle Eastern desk. I'd seen him a few times since then, twice for debrief exams and once in Kuwait when he was called in to examine some high-value targets before we started interrogating them. Now, since he was the attending physician at The Gray, I assumed he was assigned to Support Services permanently.

After Greg escorted me to the elevator, I told him I could make it the rest of the way on my own. Even though Greg's assignment included keeping an eye on me, he didn't voice any real objection to my small gesture of rebellion. However, as the elevator doors began to close, I noticed he hadn't moved. To reassure him, I gave him a small wave goodbye before the doors completely shut.

When I entered the exam room, Terry Howard was fussing over a set of empty vials used to draw blood; his head was bent low, trying to read the labels with a pair of bifocals perched precariously over his nose.

"Hey, Doc, how are—"

He juggled two of the vials, almost dropping one of them. "*Aaagh!* Titus, you startled me."

"Sorry. I thought you heard me." I waved my cane in his direction. "This thing makes a lot of noise."

"No, it doesn't," he grumbled. "And don't bother apologizing. I remember how you used to like sneaking up on people."

Terry Howard had reached his late fifties with a full head of hair, no wrinkles—except for a few lines across his forehead—and he still had the slim physique he'd had when I first met him.

His grumpy demeanor remained unchanged also.

"You don't look good at all," he groused, wrapping the blood pressure cuff around my arm.

"Well, I need a haircut."

He grunted and continued taking my vitals, making meticulous notes as he probed and prodded. Lastly, he examined what had been my busted left leg.

"It was bad, huh?"

"They said I shattered my femur and tore all the knee ligaments. It wasn't pretty."

He shook his head. "With that much damage, you were either in a car accident or playing in the NFL."

"I jumped off a very high roof. Forgot to tuck and roll."

"That would do it."

Even though he had the security clearance to do so, Howard didn't question me about the particulars of my injury—that would be the job of my debriefers. He inquired relentlessly, however, about the functioning of every part of my body.

Finally, he put his hand on my knee and gave it a twist. "Did that hurt?"

The pain was excruciating.

"Ouch. Yeah!"

"Good. Maybe the surgery didn't damage your nerves too badly."

I tried massaging the pain away. "What kind of test was that?"

He ignored me and pointed to my cane. "You'll need a few weeks of rehab to get rid of your little crutch there," he said. "After that, I can't guarantee you won't continue to have some pain, but, as I recall, pain was never a big deal to you anyway."

He reached over and touched my appendix scar.

"I'll never forget how infuriated you were with me during that training run in Raleigh when I told you your appendix was about to burst. I've never seen anyone so enraged before."

Before I could protest his recollection of events, he asked me,

"Have you learned to control that temper of yours yet?"

I wanted to give him a flippant answer, but in light of the decision I'd made one night in a tiny living room in Tehran, I decided to reply with the truth.

"I'm really trying, Doc, really trying."

Chapter 2

They left me alone for three days. At first, I figured it was because I'd arrived on Friday, and all my debriefers wanted to have a long weekend.

Later, I found out it was because Gordan Bolton—the Agency's chief of station in Turkey and the first person to greet me when Rahim released me from the trunk of his car in Dogubayazit—had suggested my bosses give me a few days off to decompress before starting my debrief.

I did nothing on Saturday except eat, sleep, and become familiar with the house. Every time I showed up in the kitchen, Martha fixed me a huge meal. For his part, Greg stayed as close to me as possible, moseying with me through the kitchen, the media room, the library, just keeping an eye on me, but willing to engage in conversation if I felt like talking.

I didn't.

I met Jim and Alex, the security officers.

Jim was an outgoing type of guy, and, like me, he was in his late forties, although his thick brown hair was already turning gray. The left side of Jim's face was disfigured by a two-inch scar running from his eye socket to his ear. However, he exuded self-confidence.

His attitude reassured me because I felt shrouded in a blanket of uncertainty.

Alex, who appeared to be in his early thirties, had curly blond hair, an acne-scarred face, and deep-set blue eyes. He barely spoke to me when we were introduced, and I had the distinct impression my presence made him nervous.

His reaction was understandable.

Covert operatives coming in from a failed mission tended to make Agency people skittish.

◆ ◆ ◆ ◆

After waking up on Sunday morning, I took my mug of thick black coffee outside, stared at the pool and gardens, and finally started asking myself some serious questions about my future.

Did I want to stay covert? Would I even be allowed to do so? After what happened in Tehran, were they going to offer me a desk job—analyst or such?

I thought about that for several minutes.

I decided I'd go crazy if I wasn't allowed out in the field.

The night before I'd left Tehran, Javad had asked me a question. I had answered him truthfully. However, what did that mean for my career now?

I was surprised by my feelings of helplessness and insecurity.

My emotional tenor reminded me of a time, ages ago, when Laura had left me for another man. I'd felt just as vulnerable then. Our divorce was one of the driving forces behind my accepting an offer to come to work for the CIA in the first place.

Did my life need to take a different turn now? Was it time to leave the Agency?

Praying about these questions felt like something I ought to do.

I bowed my head.

Nothing came.

Prayer wasn't a familiar practice in my life.

◆ ◆ ◆ ◆

By mid-morning, I was getting antsy, and, even though I was officially quarantined at The Gray until my debrief was over, I briefly considered leaving the house for a couple of hours.

I knew that the Agency's quarantine restrictions—no outside communication, television, or internet—were in place to preserve the integrity of the debrief. However, as much as I agreed with this concept in principle, trying to obey such rules always proved to be an entirely different matter altogether.

Despite my restlessness, though, I discarded my escape plans.

Instead, I wandered into the library, where I found a variety of reading choices on the shelves. There were the classics, lots of "how to" books—so I could learn about installing a toilet or making a PowerPoint presentation—and some contemporary fiction. I also found a whole shelf of religious books and different versions of the Bible.

I finally selected *A Tale of Two Cities*, *The Cambridge Guide to Astronomical Discovery*, and a Bible.

Then, I slipped off to my room.

Greg knocked on my door around one o'clock and asked me if I wanted some lunch. I followed him downstairs and into the kitchen where Martha was slicing up some roast beef.

When she saw me, she immediately picked up a remote control and turned off the flat-screen TV mounted on the wall in the breakfast nook.

Fox News Sunday was playing.

After putting down the remote, she looked over at Greg and silently mouthed an apology, "Sorry."

He waved her off.

He must have thought I hadn't heard anything.

Chris Wallace had been asking someone about Iran's nuclear program.

Alex was perched on a stool at the kitchen island wolfing down a sandwich. He gave me the once over, nodded his head, and left the room.

Greg grabbed the vacant stool, and I sat down next to him.

Martha placed a big roast beef sandwich in front of me, along with a small bowl of potato salad. "Thanks. This looks great."

She acknowledged my compliment with a smile. "You want lemonade again?"

My mouth was full, so I just nodded. A few minutes later, she placed a large icy glass in front of me.

"Greg, can I get you something?" she asked her husband.

"I'll take a cup of coffee."

After she handed him a mug, a knowing look passed between them, and, seconds later, she made an excuse and left the room.

A few minutes after she left, Greg removed a sheet of paper from his shirt pocket. "Here's the schedule for your debrief tomorrow," he said. "It looks pretty straightforward. I know you've been through this drill several times."

I took the schedule and stuffed it inside my jeans pocket without looking at it.

"You like working for the Agency, Greg?"

I wasn't sure whether it was my question or the fact I was beginning to talk, but Greg smiled when he gave me his answer. "Yes, yes, I do."

He took a sip of his coffee then gestured at his surroundings. "Obviously, this is a pretty cushy job."

"Did you ever go operational, work in the field?"

His eyes shifted slightly to the left, and he hesitated a moment before answering. I had no doubt he was weighing whether it was more important to keep me talking or follow Agency rules. He decided on the former.

However, he sounded apologetic when he answered me. "Only Level 4 action, but Martha was Level 2. We met at an Agency in-house party and got married six months later."

"So you had to transfer to Support services after you were married?"

"Yeah. There were some options, but . . ." he looked over at me, then up at a camera mounted in the ceiling, "you know how difficult it would have been to live any kind of normal life, much less see each other, if either of us had stayed in Operations."

I agreed. "It wouldn't have worked."

He nodded his head, drained the last of his coffee, and walked over to the sink, carefully rinsing out his cup.

"Did Martha have a hard time adjusting?"

Looking perplexed, he asked, "Adjusting?"

"You know. Did she miss . . ." I struggled to find the right words, "her sense of purpose about what she was doing?"

He thought about my question for a moment. "I don't think she missed the ops at first. We couldn't really talk about it, of course, but I suspected her last assignment had gotten a bit ugly. I'm sure that made the change easier." He shifted uncomfortably. "Look, Titus, you know we aren't supposed to—"

"Did she stop believing?"

There was no mistaking the anger in his voice. "Believing? You mean did she stop believing her actions were helping her country?"

"No, of course not. I'm talking about that inner calling that—"

An alarm went off—a steady *beep, beep, beep.*

Suddenly, at that moment, Jim burst through a door off the kitchen.

I had just assumed the door led to the pantry.

Assumptions can get you killed.

Beep. Beep. Beep.

Jim motioned toward me. "Follow me."

Beep. Beep. Beep.

As I headed in his direction, Martha and Alex rushed into the room.

Beep. Beep. Beep

Alex quickly walked over to a wall console and entered some numbers on a key pad.

The beeping stopped.

Seconds later, the intercom from the security gate squawked. Greg started to answer it, but Jim motioned for Martha to take it.

She took a deep breath and pressed the button.

Calmly she said, "Yes."

The female voice on the other end was high-pitched and had a Boston accent. "Oh, Martha, it's me, Teresa. I just need to drive up and have you sign this petition. It won't take a minute. I hope I'm not bothering you and Greg."

Before hearing Martha's reply, Jim ushered me past the pantry door, through a false wall at the back of the pantry and into a large room. It contained a wall of security monitors, computers, and several different kinds of communications equipment.

On one of the monitors, I saw a very thin woman dressed in a pair of black slacks and a yellow blouse. She was standing outside the security gate speaking into the intercom. As I watched, she got back inside her Mercedes and waited for the gate to slide open.

Jim was watching the other video feeds from around the grounds, while also keeping an eye on a nearby computer screen as it rapidly scanned through thousands of images using the Agency's facial recognition software. As soon as a match for Teresa came up on the computer screen, he hit the button for the gate to open.

Speaking into his wrist mike, he said, "We have benign contact. Repeat. Benign contact."

Alex keyed back, "Copy. Benign contact."

Jim looked over at me. "She's just a neighbor. She called Martha earlier in the week to see if she would sign a petition to keep the city from cutting down a tree on the right-of-way. It's creating a traffic hazard." He shook his head. "Teresa's a champion of lost causes."

I took the chance to look around.

I felt sure the door on the opposite wall led to a safe room. Once a person was inside, the room could not be breached—at least not easily.

Jim glanced up at me. "Yeah, that's the safe room, but we're good right here. Martha knows how to deal with this situation."

We watched as Martha opened the front door and invited Teresa inside the foyer. They were smiling and chatting like actors in a silent movie.

Everything seemed fine, but I found myself wishing I were armed.

Along with Jim, I scanned the monitors showing the video from the grounds.

"Where's the feed from the pool house?" I asked, nervously.

He pointed to a split screen. "It's this one. It's shared with the feed from the garage."

We went back to watching the action on the screen, and I asked him to turn the audio on.

Martha and Teresa moved into the living room where Greg joined them. He was carrying a book, trying to look as if Teresa's arrival had interrupted his reading. He and Martha sat down on the sofa, and, using Greg's book for a hard surface, they signed Teresa's petition.

As they played out their deceptive scenario, I could see the differences in their operational styles firsthand.

Greg's face was stiff, devoid of any expression; his hand movements were jerky and nervous, and his voice was just a bit too loud. However, Martha appeared relaxed, even comfortable, as if she were enjoying herself. Her body posture mirrored Teresa's movements, and she stayed in sync with Teresa's conversational pattern.

After a few minutes, Jim and I watched as the three of them walked toward the front door together.

"She's consistently good," Jim said. "Greg's always twitchy, though."

My nerves eased up, and I turned away from the security console and walked around the room, poking my nose into a wall cabinet, running my hand over some books on a bookshelf.

"The gun safe is downstairs."

I turned and smiled at him. "I'm that obvious, huh?"

"I've been in your shoes, that's all."

He opened the door to a cabinet and took out a pistol.

"I keep an extra firearm in here. It would have been yours if our security had been breached."

"Good to know."

He quickly put the gun back in its hiding place.

"You didn't hear it from me though." He made a sweeping motion with his hand. "Of course, no one hears anything in here."

I made a mental note of that information. Since everything was being monitored throughout the safe house, at least the communications room was one place I could have a frank conversation without fear of blowback.

I turned my attention back to the monitors and watched Teresa pull her car into the street. When the gates closed behind her, Jim gave Alex the all clear.

I looked around the room one last time.

I said, "Well, I guess I'd better get back out there."

Jim flipped a switch to unlock the door leading through the pantry to the kitchen.

As I walked past him, he put his hand out to stop me.

"Look, Titus, I know I'm not supposed to know as much about you as I do, but there's always talk, you know that. Well . . . I want you to know, I'm here if you need anything or if you'd just like to talk to someone."

"Thanks, Jim."

I started toward the door, but then I turned back and said, "Could I ask you a question?"

"Of course."

"What's the most important thing in the world to you?"

At first, he seemed taken aback by my question.

Then, he quickly recovered and said, "I'd have to say it's my family. My wife and two kids mean everything to me."

I nodded.

"Why would you ask me that?"

"An asset asked me that question just before he was murdered."

He gave me a look of understanding.

"So, how did you answer him?"

"I never got the chance."

CHAPTER 3

On Monday morning, I awoke with a sense of relief mingled with trepidation—similar to the way I usually felt when I was about to embark on a new mission. However, unlike most of my operations, my Agency debriefing should only take a couple of days—depending on who was on the debriefing team and how they were interpreting my narrative.

When I thought about who might be assigned to my debriefing team, I decided it was time to shave off my beard. I also decided, after studying my face in the bathroom mirror, that Terry Howard was wrong; I didn't look that bad. Granted, I wasn't George Clooney handsome, but who was?

Years ago, someone had told me I was a pretty good-looking guy. Since then, no one had told me otherwise.

My trainers at The Farm had described my face as one that "blended." They considered that a good thing. Put me in a restaurant, a bus station, a mosque, and I blended right in. I didn't draw attention.

Only, as it turned out in Tehran, one time I did.

After taking a quick shower, I put on the clothing supplied for me by Support Services—a pair of dark slacks and a blue oxford shirt. My debriefers would be in very formal business attire, but I knew if I looked halfway decent and appeared to be in my right mind, that's all they expected of me. Unlike Bud Thorsen—who had a nervous breakdown after a two-year stint in Yemen and had arrived at his debriefing sessions in his pajamas—I did not want a transfer to a desk job.

At least, I didn't think so.

After I got dressed, I tried praying again. Javad and his wife, Darya, had told me it was easy, just like talking to someone. They had often prayed for me while I was living with them in Tehran, and I suspected they continued to pray for me even now.

I bowed my head and told God I wasn't looking forward to spilling my guts at the debrief. I admitted I was uncertain about my future, and it was eating away at me, and I also asked him to help me control my temper. When I finished, I decided Javad was right—praying wasn't really that hard.

Because I had no desire to stand around and make small talk with any Agency personnel, I skipped Martha's breakfast and remained in my room until Greg knocked on my door.

Then, I headed down to the festivities.

◆ ◆ ◆ ◆

I arrived at the lower level conference room just as Martha was coming out the door.

She gave me a fleeting smile and whispered, "I left you some cinnamon rolls. Make sure you get some." As I held the door open for her, she added, "There's also a carafe of lemonade for you."

I whispered back. "Thanks."

Although the conference table in the room could easily seat ten people, only four chairs were occupied. Douglas Carlton, my official handler and the operations officer for my mission, was seated on the right side of the table all alone.

He would be in charge of the debrief.

He was reading from a stack of papers, and I knew he was probably studying the overnight cables. Carlton was someone who prided himself on being a "detail person," and he would inform everyone of this organizational attribute at least twice in every meeting.

Carlton was bald-headed with enormous brown eyes that grew larger whenever he disagreed with something being said. He was a meticulous dresser. Today he wore a gray, pinstriped suit, long-sleeved white shirt—with the hint of a cuff showing—and a pastel-colored tie adorned with tiny, silver geometric designs.

He looked like a Wall Street banker.

Ours was a love/hate relationship.

He caught a glimpse of me out of the corner of his eye and quickly got up from his chair and started toward me. I met him halfway. He grabbed my outstretched hand and put his other hand on my shoulder, squeezing hard.

Speaking each word as if it were a sentence all by itself, he said, "So. Good. To. See. You." He pumped my hand for several seconds. "You look . . ." he paused and looked me over from head to toe, "amazingly well after all you've been through."

"I've gotten some rest," I said, "and I've been eating like a horse since I got here."

"Good." He pointed toward a credenza where an assortment of snacks and drinks were laid out. "Why don't you get yourself something to eat, and we'll get started."

As I turned to go, he patted me on the back. "I understand you didn't have any breakfast this morning."

Carlton always wanted you to know he knew more about you than you thought he did.

This personality trait accounted for the hate part of our relationship.

I grabbed a cinnamon roll and a cup of coffee and took my assigned seat at the head of the table. Carlton was seated to my left. He was distributing stacks of documents to the other three debriefers who were seated across the table from him and to my right. They had not been speaking to each other when I entered the room, and they remained focused on other tasks as I sat down.

The farthest person from me was Katherine Broward, the Agency's chief strategic analyst. She was intent on texting or entering some information on her iPhone, and she had not turned her head or met my gaze since I'd entered the room.

Katherine was also dressed in a gray business suit, but, unlike Carlton, she wore a frilly red blouse underneath her jacket. Since she had been with the Agency for less than 10 years, I put her age at around thirty-five, but discerning a woman's age was difficult for me. Discerning beauty, however, was an entirely different matter, and I knew Katherine was a very beautiful woman. She had long, honey-blond hair, green eyes, and a rather prominent chin.

At one time, Katherine and I had tried to have a relationship.

However, I'd only managed one lunch, followed by dinner a week later. Then, I was off to Afghanistan. I don't remember the excuse Katherine gave me when I asked her out upon my return, but I do remember thinking it was a very believable lie.

"Sorry, I'm late."

Every head turned as Robert Ira entered the conference room.

As I observed the look on Carlton's face, I realized he, like everyone else, seemed surprised to see the Deputy Director of Operations show up in person for the debriefing of a covert intelligence officer.

Carlton quickly got up from his chair. "Deputy Ira, this is a pleasant surprise. I didn't realize the Director was sending someone over for the debrief."

Ira placed a large black briefcase on the conference table. "I hope this isn't an inconvenience."

"No. No. Not at all," Carlton said. "Here, take this seat. I'll move over."

Ira eased his large bulky body into the chair just vacated by Carlton. Then, he opened his briefcase and rummaged around inside it a moment, finally removing a laptop computer.

The Deputy's pudgy face, combined with his stringy gray hair and bulbous red nose, made him appear more like a cartoon character than a high-ranking intelligence administrator. However, I'd always suspected his looks were a bit of cunning camouflage for his devious but brilliant mind. In his position, an unappealing appearance went hand-in-hand with an unappealing job.

Robert Ira was the point man for the CIA's Director of Operations. He was sent out to look for operational and political minefields that could blow up in the Agency's face. To that end, he was tasked with assessing the successes and failures of an operation and of evaluating its financial gains and losses. His bottom-line reports to the Director were both feared and cheered. They could bring either curses or blessings on the agent involved.

I had been the recipient of both.

However, Ira seldom left Agency headquarters, preferring instead to sit in his office gathering data from operational officers, reading reports, making phone calls, and holding endless meetings. His presence at my debrief signaled someone was definitely worried about some aspect of Operation Torchlight.

Those worries were well founded.

Carlton cleared his throat and addressed the room. "First, I'd like to begin by making some introductions, then, I'll take care of the preliminaries, and, finally," Carlton paused and glanced over at me, "we'll hear from Titus."

That was partly true. They would indeed hear from me, but I, in turn, would hear from them. That's the way an operational debrief worked: I would tell my story; they would ask me questions. Some of those questions would be intended to show how much they knew, and how little I really knew.

I didn't mind that.

I've never minded finding out what others thought I didn't know.

Carlton began his introductions.

"Titus, I believe you're already acquainted with Katherine." Carlton gave her a nod. She, in turn, gave me just the briefest hint of a smile. "You're also acquainted with Mr. Haddadi, who's here to help us with any language and cultural issues we might encounter today."

Komeil Haddadi had been a high-ranking scientist in Iran's nuclear program until five years ago when he had walked into the American Embassy in London and defected—much to everyone's surprise and delight. Carlton was a member of the team who had spent several weeks interrogating him, and I'd never heard Carlton call him anything but Mr. Haddadi. However, since the two of us had spent considerable time together two years ago, while prepping for my assignment in Iran, I'd always called him Komeil.

Komeil reached across the table and clasped my hand in both of his. "So good to have you back."

As Komeil gave me a broad smile, I was reminded of pictures I'd seen of the Shah of Iran. He resembled the Shah enough to have been his brother.

Carlton finished up his introductions. "Sitting next to Mr. Haddadi is Tony Fowler. He's our outside observer for this debriefing session."

Fowler was an African-American with square, wire-rimmed glasses and a short, neat haircut. I noticed he kept fiddling with his iPad, even while Carlton was introducing everyone.

I wasn't acquainted with Tony Fowler, but we exchanged perfunctory nods.

Because Fowler was the outside observer for my debrief, it didn't surprise me we'd never met before. In fact, had we known each other, he could not have been the outside observer.

All operational debriefing sessions were assigned a person from another division, someone who had not been involved in the mission itself and who did not know the covert intelligence officer being debriefed. The reasoning behind this rule was that an outside observer brought a new perspective and provided insights not otherwise apparent to the operational team. The Director had instituted this regulation at the urging of a congressional oversight committee ten years ago, but the responsibility for choosing the outside observer had been turned over to the DDO, Robert Ira.

In my opinion, outside observers asked far too many questions during a debrief. This slowed down the whole process and interfered with the intelligence officer's flow of thought in narrating the events of an operation. Such irrelevant interrogations primarily occurred because a debrief was an invaluable opportunity for an observer to delve into operations beyond his or her intelligence scope, giving that person a treasure trove of information. Such knowledge was highly coveted and served as a powerful commodity within the walls of the Agency.

Carlton turned to his left and addressed Ira. "Once again, let me say how privileged we are to have you in the room today, Deputy Ira.

I believe you've met everyone here before?"

He smiled at Katherine and glanced briefly at the rest of us. "Yes, I have."

"I'll begin with the formalities," Carlton said, "and let me remind everyone that these sessions are being recorded."

Carlton cleared his throat yet again. When he spoke, his voice was slightly stilted.

"Session One. This is Operations Officer, Douglas Carlton, in the intelligence debrief of Titus Alan Ray, Level 1 covert operative for Operation Torchlight."

He pointed a finger in my direction. "Begin the narrative."

◆ ◆ ◆ ◆

"Two years ago, I entered Iran on a Swiss passport. My cover name was Hammid Salimi, the son of an Iranian watchmaker and a Swiss businesswoman. My legend was solid. I was in Tehran to open up a market for my parents' line of luxury watches and jewelry. The contacts I made among the elite in the Iranian regime were to serve as the prime recruiting ground for a cadre of assets Operations hoped would help fund the Iranian opposition and topple the government."

Not surprisingly, Fowler was the first committee member to break into my narrative. However, his eyes barely left his iPad as he threw out his questions.

"Aren't most wealthy Iranians in lock-step with the regime?" he asked. "How was such an operation even feasible?"

Carlton responded immediately. "Yes, Tony, that's an excellent question, and it's one I'll be happy to answer."

Carlton picked up a set of documents on the table, although he didn't refer to them immediately.

"All our data pointed to a great disaffection among the upper echelon of Iranian society. We heard from a variety of sources," he gestured toward Komeil, "including Mr. Haddadi, who indicated that the elite in Iran might be willing to help the opposition, despite continually receiving incentives from the government."

Mr. Haddadi shifted in his chair and opened his mouth, but before he could utter a word, Carlton began reading from the set of papers he was holding. He'd chosen several sections describing the mind-numbing psychological details about the thinking of Iran's upper class.

As his voice droned on, I knew I wasn't the only person in the room feeling sleepy.

Finally, when I couldn't stand it any longer, I interrupted him. "I recruited four assets within six months and two more the next year."

Fowler looked up from his iPad.

I added defiantly, "It was obviously a workable operation."

Fowler peered at me over the tops of his glasses, studying me for a few seconds. Then, he said, "Duly noted."

Perhaps trying to lower the testosterone in the room, Katherine spoke up.

"Our product from these recruits was extremely beneficial," she said. "Not only was Titus able to penetrate this closed community, he was also able to gain access into—"

"Well, let's not get ahead of ourselves," Carlton said, obviously trying to regain control of the meeting. "Titus, continue the narrative."

I spent almost an hour explaining how I went about identifying my targets by developing business relationships, cultivating ties in banking circles, and socializing with the affluent in Iranian society. When I got into some of the more specific details of the money I was spending to live such a lavish lifestyle, Deputy Ira started rapidly typing on his laptop.

I did not take that as a good sign.

Katherine, probably thinking the same thing, asked a question that prodded me on to a different topic. "Titus, wasn't the purchase of your apartment the reason you were able to develop a friendship with Amir Madani?"

At the mention of Amir's name, Fowler's head shot up and Ira suddenly stopped typing.

I was puzzled at their sudden interest.

"Correct," I said. "I was sitting at an outdoor café with Farid, one of my recruits, when an acquaintance of his stopped by our table. Farid introduced his friend to me as Amir."

As I described my chance encounter with Amir, I noticed a slight tic had developed below Fowler's left eye.

"I immediately recognized the man as Amir Madani," I said, "one of Iran's nuclear scientists, so I decided to use Farid to see if I could get closer to him."

"How?" Fowler asked.

"Pardon me?"

"How were you able to recognize him?"

"Well, because . . ." I hesitated for only a split second but it was just enough time for him to hit me with a barrage of other questions before I could finish answering his first one.

"Since your operational mandate was to cultivate assets to finance the opposition, what was your interest in this Amir?" he asked. "Your warrant didn't include targeting Iran's scientists, did it?"

I suddenly found myself extremely curious about Tony Fowler.

Because he was the outside observer on the committee, the position he held in the Agency was unknown to me. He could be employed in any section of Operations. Of course, everyone else in the room, except possibly Komeil, knew the name of his division.

For my part, I was beginning to suspect which door his key card might open.

However, if I were guessing correctly, it meant someone at the Agency had deliberately sabotaged my mission in Tehran.

Carlton immediately spoke up. "Of course, I authorized it."

Fowler seemed stunned. "You did?"

For several seconds, Fowler seemed to be grappling for another question. Finally, he asked, "When?"

Carlton's eyes grew wider. "When? You mean you want the actual date?" A puzzled look passed over Carlton's face. Moments later, he looked over at Ira, as if hoping the DDO might be able to clear up his confusion.

However, the deputy immediately turned his attention to his laptop, ignoring Carlton's bewildered stare.

Fowler was adamant when he answered Carlton. "No, I don't want a date. I want a timeline."

Carlton shuffled through his notes. While I had no idea what was bothering him about Fowler's question, I could tell he was simply stalling for time.

Fowler continued questioning Carlton. "Did you authorize contact before or after Titus recognized him? I want to understand how it was that Titus knew this man in the first place. There are thousands of people walking the streets of Iran. It seems odd that he would be able to—"

"I showed him pictures," Komeil said, barging into the exchange.

Fowler looked surprised. "Why would you do that?"

"Look, Tony," I said, before Komeil could answer him, "Perhaps I should have explained how I went about preparing for this mission. My oversight may have caused you some misunderstanding, and I take full responsibility for that. Let me back up and tell you about my preparation for Operation Torchlight."

I noticed a smile flicker across Katherine's face, and I wondered if she knew I was simply trying to buy Carlton time to resolve his confusion.

Fowler removed his glasses and began massaging his temples. "Sure, why don't you do that?"

I launched into a myriad of details explaining how Legends—the branch of Support Services responsible for creating false identities— had prepared my background, my credentials, and my entry into Iran. Then, I inundated Fowler with the kind of research I undertook prior to a mission. Finally, I described how Komeil and I had worked together to enable me a quick integration into Iranian society.

"I met with Komeil three times a week for two months," I said. "We only spoke Farsi when we were together. When we—"

"Why are you so fluent in Farsi?" Fowler asked. He sounded surprisingly accusatory. "Were you ever in Iran before this assignment?"

I turned to Carlton for approval. He gave me a dismissive wave of his hand. "Go ahead," he said, while continuing to look through his stack of documents.

"No, I had never been to Iran before this mission. And the language? It's just a gift. It doesn't take me long to acquire fluency in any language."

I started to elaborate about how many languages I spoke, but Fowler had no real need to know. An operational debriefing was not so much about the operative as it was about the operation. Tony Fowler was not cleared in this setting to know more about me than Carlton wanted him to know.

"Komeil briefed me on some prominent people I should get to know in Tehran," I said. "As I was studying the photographs of these people, I came across several group shots he had taken with some of his scientific colleagues while they were attending a conference together. We talked about their backgrounds, and that's how I recognized Amir Madani when I saw him that day."

I twisted open a bottle of water sitting in front of me and took a very long drink.

As I drank, Fowler appeared impatient, anxious for me to continue my narrative. I knew he wanted an explanation of why I'd decided to seek authorization to start courting Amir when my mission's objective didn't include contact with one of Iran's nuclear scientist. For some reason, such information appeared to be extremely important to him.

However, I placed the empty bottle of water back on the table and remained silent.

I waited for Fowler to ask me the question again. I needed to hear his exact words and sentence structure, to catch the nuance, and to watch his facial expression.

As the silence grew, Carlton made an elaborate show of checking his watch. "Titus," he said, "let's break for lunch and resume in two hours."

Carlton watched as Tony Fowler hurriedly left the room. Then, when the door slammed shut, he turned to Ira. "Deputy, could we have lunch together?"

I had no idea where the two of them were going for lunch, but wherever it was, I knew Carlton wasn't leaving there until Deputy Ira had served him up some satisfactory answers. When it came to getting answers, Carlton was like a kid bugging his mom for a new toy—he would never give up until he got what he wanted.

This personality trait accounted for the love part of our relationship.

CHAPTER 4

Since I wasn't allowed to leave the grounds until clearing my debrief, I took the plate of food Martha had prepared for me and escaped onto the patio, sitting at a table beside the Olympic-size swimming pool.

It was a beautiful sunny day in April, and although the wind was chilly, I wanted the freedom of being outdoors too much to care about the temperature.

As I ate my chicken salad sandwich, I decided not to think about the dynamics occurring inside my debrief. Instead, I watched two groundskeepers cleaning out a flowerbed. They appeared to be enjoying each other's company, laughing and talking together as they worked.

However, the longer I watched them, the more I realized I wasn't just showing them passing curiosity. On a professional level, I was assessing them, scrutinizing their movements, trying to determine if they presented any real danger to me.

Since The Gray was encased in a secured environment, my obsessive exercise made me wonder if I'd been living the clandestine life too long.

Was it mentally healthy to be so suspicious? Was my wariness a sure indicator I needed to get out? Should I take the initiative and ask to be transferred to a desk job?

Yet, being a covert intelligence operative was the only thing I knew how to do, and I did it very well. I knew that.

As a kid growing up in Flint, Michigan, I thought I wanted to be a police officer or maybe an FBI agent. My parents never discouraged me, nor, for that matter, did they encourage me to pursue law enforcement. In fact, my dad, Gerald, who worked on the assembly line at GM, didn't pay much attention to me at all. In some ways, he was the typical alcoholic dad. He worked on the line all day, and then he drank himself to sleep every night. He wasn't mean, and he didn't mistreat my mom or my sister. He was simply emotionally absent from our family.

My mother, Sharon, who was a high school science teacher, relied on empirical evidence to explain her husband's behavior. "When Gerald came home from Vietnam, he was a broken man," she often told people. "He saw way too many horrible things over there, and it's haunted him ever since."

Perhaps my father experienced the most horrifying aspects of that war, but he was never willing to talk to me about any of them, and I certainly tried often enough. As a young boy, I asked him endless questions about the Army. What was like to be shot at? How did it feel to see someone die? However, his answers were always vague or monosyllabic. As a teenager, his attitude infuriated me, and we exchanged heated words on a regular basis. By the time I left for college, we were barely speaking.

As expected, my relationship with my father was a topic the Agency psychiatrists discussed with me when I applied for the CIA. At the end of those intense sessions, I finally realized my failure to bond with my father was the motivation behind my willingness to embrace Laura Hudson and her family.

Laura and I had met during my first month at the University of Michigan. Within a few weeks of being introduced, we were spending all of our time together, and, during one weekend in November, she invited me home to meet her parents.

Roman and Cynthia Hudson were welcoming, gracious people. I was immediately drawn to them, especially Roman, who owned a hardware store in a strip mall in Ann Arbor and started calling me "son" as soon as we were introduced.

Instead of returning home for Christmas during my freshman year, I spent my entire two-week break with Laura's family in Ann Arbor. It was then I learned Roman had also been in Vietnam, but there was a big difference between him and my father—he was more than willing to talk about what he'd done over there.

The first time Roman had mentioned Southeast Asia was when Laura and I had stopped by the hardware store on Christmas Eve to see if we could help with the holiday rush. Laura's mother, Cynthia, was working as a cashier, so Laura had opened up another cash register, while I went to find Roman. I located him at the back of the store in the sporting goods section where he was showing a gun to a customer.

Because I'd never been around firearms before, I watched in awe at how easily he handled the weapon, stripping it down, explaining its features, and then putting the whole thing back together in the blink of an eye. Roman noticed my fascination at his expertise, and when the customer left, he immediately began telling me stories of his time in Vietnam working for the CIA.

Laughing at himself, he said, "They called us spooks back then."

For Christmas, he gave me my first weapon, a .22 revolver, and I spent the rest of the week at the gun range. The following year, during my Spring break, two important things occurred: I asked Laura to marry me and Roman gave me a Smith & Wesson .357 magnum.

I married Laura the following June.

For a wedding present, her parents gave us the down payment on a small house near the campus. However, between both of us going to school full-time and working at our part-time jobs, I barely remembered living there. Besides that, I chose to spend most of my free time with Roman.

Roman not only continued teaching me everything he knew about weaponry, he also tutored me in the rudiments of the tradecraft he was taught during his brief time working for the Agency. I hadn't made a conscious decision to join the CIA yet, but before starting my junior year of college, I switched my major from business to international relations with a minor in languages.

By our second year of marriage, Laura was growing increasingly unhappy about my relationship with her dad. Even though I knew Laura hated all the time I was spending with Roman, I refused to change at all. When we would argue—which was often—I'd lose my temper and say incredibly cruel things to her.

Eventually, Laura found someone else.

The day she asked me for a divorce, she said, "You didn't fall in love with me, Titus; you fell in love with my dad."

She was right, of course.

At first, I blamed the failure of my marriage on my disappointing family life. Later, I realized when Laura and I had met, I'd been sinking in a sea of uncertainty. Then, out of the fog, Roman had appeared to me as a lighthouse, and I'd been drawn to him as my only means of rescue.

Perhaps not surprisingly, a week after signing the final divorce papers, I was talking to a CIA recruiter.

◆ ◆ ◆ ◆

After finishing up my sandwich, I went back inside and put my dishes in the kitchen sink. The room was empty, so I faced the ceiling camera, raised my arm, and made a circling motion with my forefinger. Within a few seconds, Jim came through the pantry door.

"Got a problem?" he asked.

"Just a question."

He gestured for me to follow him, and we went back to his lair in the communications room. As soon as he sat down in front of the security monitors, I saw him glance up at the feed coming from the kitchen video. He noted the time on a yellow pad.

Then he pointed toward a chair. "Have a seat."

The chair he indicated faced a wall of wide-screen monitors displaying video from several different news agencies. The headlines scrolling across the screens indicated something newsworthy was happening in North Korea, and I was sorely tempted to feast my eyes on every word and satisfy my curiosity.

However, I resisted. I knew I was about to break one of the house rules, and one broken rule a day was my self-imposed quota.

Jim looked amused when I repositioned the chair so I was facing him instead of the screens.

"What's your question?"

"Before I ask it, I want you to know I'm assuming several things, which will be obvious to you when I ask the question. If I'm assuming incorrectly, and you don't want to answer the question, then know for certain I won't think less of you."

He considered my statement for a couple of seconds, and then he nodded. "Okay."

"Tony Fowler."

Jim blinked his eyes several times.

I continued with my question. "Have I been playing around in his backyard?"

This time Jim's reaction was to stare at me without blinking. He did this for what seemed like a long time, but it was probably only twenty seconds or so.

I knew he'd been monitoring the feed from the video in the debriefing room during the morning session. That was his job. He could also lose his job if he revealed the identity of the outside observer to me.

However, if Jim had truly "been in my shoes," as he'd indicated to me on Sunday, then he also knew the position I was in with Tony Fowler. He understood how valuable this little bit of information was to me as I continued my narrative in the afternoon session.

He continued to hold my gaze.

I waited.

"Yes," he finally said.

I suddenly realized I'd been holding my breath. "Thanks."

"No problem."

He pointed toward the security feed from the kitchen. "When you go back out there, I'll run this back and erase it when you move away from the kitchen sink."

"That should do it."

◆ ◆ ◆ ◆

I still had some time before my debrief was scheduled to resume, so I slipped upstairs to my bedroom. I needed a few minutes alone to get my head around what I'd discovered.

The information Jim had just confirmed for me was that Tony Fowler was head of the Nuclear Security Division (NSD). Now, it made sense why he had reacted so strongly when I'd mentioned meeting the Iranian nuclear scientist, Amir Madani.

Fowler's portfolio at NSD included running agents in any country seeking nuclear weapons, and he should have been well acquainted—at least by name—with all of Iran's nuclear personnel. Fowler's division had a number of covert operatives in Iran responsible for developing assets in their nuclear program. Perhaps one of them had even tried to recruit Amir.

Of course, from a geographic standpoint, having such a broad scope to his job description meant Fowler was required to co-ordinate his operations with other regional divisions. Otherwise, an operative from the Middle East Division and an operative from NSD might be targeting the same asset.

For example, imagine that Carlton had a covert intelligence officer in place in Tehran. Now imagine this officer had accidently met a nuclear scientist at a café and decided to develop him as an asset. In such a scenario, the correct Agency procedure called for Carlton to inform NSD of said encounter. However, Carlton could not just walk across the hall to the NSD and discuss the matter with Tony Fowler in person. No, the Agency would never allow such a direct communication between divisions. Instead, protocol called for Carlton to inform Robert Ira. Ira, in turn, was responsible for notifying Fowler and the NSD that an agent wished to pursue contact with a nuclear scientist.

If Fowler had no objection—such as he was pursuing the asset himself or had some information on him that precluded contact—Ira would then relay the message to Carlton, who would authorize his intelligence officer to develop the asset.

Now, the picture was becoming clearer.

Either Carlton had never notified Robert Ira of my request to pursue Amir—which was unlikely because Carlton had emphatically affirmed in the morning session that he'd authorized my contact—or Ira had never informed Fowler that a Middle Eastern operative was asking permission to target a nuclear scientist.

Thinking back on Fowler's behavior in the morning session, I came to the conclusion Fowler had not known about my pursuit of Amir as a CIA asset until I'd mentioned it. Was that the reason Robert Ira was at my debriefing? Had he failed to inform Fowler I was pursuing Amir Madani?

If so, why didn't the DDO follow the correct procedure and coordinate with Fowler's office on such a critical issue? For the whole field of operations to work smoothly, there had to be cooperation among the different divisions. Otherwise, operatives and assets would overlap, and it would be chaotic and dangerous for everyone, especially in a hostile environment like Iran.

Iran was one of the most difficult countries in the world in which to gather intelligence. Civilians and military personnel were taught— by the propaganda arm of Iran's elite Revolutionary Guards Corps— to be constantly on the alert for "infiltrators" and "enemies" who wanted to penetrate all aspects of society so they could exploit Iran's "secrets."

In such an atmosphere, human intelligence gathering, especially in regards to Iran's nuclear program, was abysmal—so sparse as to be non-existent. Government agencies were forced to rely on satellite surveillance or the occasional defector, like Komeil Haddadi, to obtain even an inkling of what was going on inside Iran's nuclear community.

Such a shortage of intelligence had been foremost on my mind when I'd originally contacted Carlton about checking out Amir and possibly targeting him as a source. Since the NSD had done such a lousy job of finding and developing assets, now I wondered if Robert Ira had taken things a step further and simply cut the NSD division out of the loop entirely, never even informing Fowler that an intelligence officer—namely, me—had requested permission to pursue an Iranian scientist as a potential asset.

If my suspicions were correct and Ira had given Carlton the green light without informing Tony Fowler, then he'd blatantly disregarded crucial inter-division communication and had jeopardized my life.

Far more importantly, his decision had contributed to—if not caused—the murder of my assets.

Now, I had a big decision to make.

CHAPTER 5

I stepped into the bathroom and splashed some cold water on my face. Then, I sat down in the overstuffed chair in front of the bedroom's fireplace and mapped out how I was going to proceed with my narrative in the afternoon session.

I could go back down to my debrief and spin my tale in such a way everyone would be placated, and no one would be blamed for the debacle of my mission.

If I took that route, I would have to minimize my contact with Amir and blame the rolling up of my network on my sloppy tradecraft. While distasteful, such a strategy would probably satisfy everyone.

Of course, using this tactic meant I would have to weave a tapestry of lies.

That would not be a problem for me.

Lying is second nature and I do it very well.

Then I considered the alternative—telling the truth.

However, I wasn't sure what the repercussions of such a decision would be. Was it even a viable option?

Whatever I decided to do, I knew my future at the Agency was about to change dramatically.

I'd been preparing myself for such a change from the moment Javad's family had come into their living room to pray for me just hours before I was to make my escape from Tehran. That night, Javad and Darya, their teenage son, Mansoor, along with Rahim, had joined hands and prayed a beautiful, fervent prayer for my well-being and safe travel through the mountains of Iran to safety in Turkey.

Javad, along with several of his relatives, owned a fruit and vegetable stand in one of Tehran's open-air markets, and Darya was a nurse who worked at a neighborhood clinic. I had been forced to live with these Iranian Christians for three months in a safe house, while hiding out from Iran's Revolutionary Guard Corps.

Each night, from my bed in a corner of their tiny living room, I had observed them at their kitchen table praying and reading their Bible together before going to bed. However, they didn't keep their beliefs private. In fact, they seemed to have an insatiable desire to share their faith—especially with me. They did this even though their pastor, Youcef, was in prison because of his proselytizing. However, they were doing something even more dangerous. Not only were they proselytizing, they were also harboring an American spy and facilitating his escape from Iran.

Before leaving them, I had thanked them profusely for their help. I had also commended them because, even though they were required to go to work every day and pretend they were just harmless Iranian citizens, they had practiced excellent tradecraft in keeping me safe.

Javad had responded to my gratitude by saying, "Oh, Hammid, it's not difficult for us to do this because we remember the words of Jesus. He said we were to be like sheep living among the wolves. He told us to be as shrewd as snakes and as innocent as doves."

Now, as I left my room to face my debriefers once again, I decided those words—to be both shrewd and innocent—might be good advice for me as well.

In reality, when it came to events in Tehran, I was both.

◆ ◆ ◆ ◆

Deputy Ira and Carlton were huddled together on one side of the table when I reentered the conference room. They were engaged in a whispered conversation, and from their body language, it appeared the two men had come to some sort of mutually satisfactory understanding.

I decided not to disturb them.

Instead, I walked over to the refreshment table where Katherine was pouring herself a cup of coffee.

"Enjoy your lunch?" I asked.

She tore open a packet of sweetener and dumped it into her coffee.

"I had a delicious salad, thank you. How about you?"

"I had a chicken salad sandwich with a side of contemplation."

She smiled. "I'll bet you did." Gesturing toward my leg, she asked, "Are you feeling okay? How's your leg?"

"It's getting there."

Katherine cut her eyes over to where Carlton and Ira were standing. Then, in a half whisper, she said, "I'm sorry for what happened to you, Titus."

I didn't reply because I thought she was about to add something to her statement. Instead, she abruptly turned and walked away, taking her seat at the conference table.

I poured myself a glass of lemonade and followed her over to the table, stopping to exchange greetings with Komeil. As I sat down, I realized Tony Fowler was not in the room.

I quickly ran through the possibilities of what Fowler's absence might mean.

I immediately discarded the notion he was simply playing hooky, because since the debriefing process had already begun, it would take an act of God or the intervention of the Director himself to get Fowler out of his selection as the outside observer.

However, since he must have realized the DDO had not followed the correct protocol in regards to Amir, he could have contacted Legal during lunch and stirred up a real hornet's nest. In that case, I fully expected Fowler to return to the debrief in the company of two or three other suits. If that happened, I would simply take my place in the audience, because, at that point, the ensuing confrontation between Ira and Fowler would be center stage.

As I was about to consider another possibility, Fowler walked in.

He was alone.

Rushing over to his seat, he said, "Sorry. Traffic was a mess."

Carlton placed the document he'd been holding on the pile of papers in front of him. Using both hands, he carefully aligned the edges of the stack. Finally, he looked up and addressed the group.

"We're running behind schedule," he said, "but before Titus begins his narrative again, let me explain how I like to run these debriefing sessions."

He looked down at his stack of papers again.

Nothing had moved.

"I'm a detail kind of person," he continued, "and that's why I believe in taking the time to tease out the little things. Sometimes," he looked across the table at Fowler, "it's the little things that really matter."

Fowler was giving Carlton his full attention. He hadn't even opened his iPad.

Carlton turned and addressed me directly. "Titus, go back and review for us what you knew about Amir Madani before you requested permission to approach him. Once you do that, explain what occurred after the two of you were introduced."

I nodded.

Once again, Deputy Ira opened up his laptop. Only this time, he didn't touch his keyboard. Instead, he peered across the table at Tony Fowler.

Did Fowler know he was in the deputy's crosshairs?

I would know soon enough.

◆ ◆ ◆ ◆

"Session Two. This is Operations Officer, Douglas Carlton, in the intelligence debrief of Titus Alan Ray, Level 1 covert operative, for Operation Torchlight."

I began the afternoon session. "When Komeil and I were discussing the backgrounds of the nuclear scientists who appeared in his conference photographs, I was intrigued by Amir Madani because he was young, he was rich, and Komeil said he was new school. I memorized his face because he seemed to be exactly the type of asset we'd profiled in the operation. Granted, since he was a scientist he wasn't really in the category of Iran's elite. However, that was the very thing that made him so interesting to me. He was both wealthy and a prominent scientist in the nuclear energy field."

"What do you mean by new school?" Katherine asked.

I smiled at her. "That's a good question."

She smiled back.

"As I understand it, the younger scientists in today's modern Iran aren't happy with their government's dependence on other nations for nuclear research and development. The regime's deference to Russia is a perfect example of this. To put it simply, they see relinquishing control of any aspect of Iran's nuclear capabilities as old school. The younger bucks are eager to show how brilliant they are in their own right."

"It's also economics," Komeil added. "Too much money goes out of Iran for such technology, and the young people of today want a strong economy so they can buy more Western music and clothes. The youth in today's Iran do not know of hardship. I can tell you many stories of how—"

Carlton cut him off. "Thank you, Mr. Haddadi."

Then, Carlton turned to me. "So, Titus, what happened after you met Amir Madani?"

"I didn't contact anyone at the Agency immediately," I said. "I wanted to make sure it was going to be worth the extra effort on my part to approach him. I had my hands full developing the six assets I was running, and I didn't want to take Amir on unless it was going to pay big dividends."

Carlton nodded. "And how did you go about doing that?"

I spent a few minutes explaining about my efforts to discover where Amir lived and worked. Then I described the way I went about putting him under surveillance for several days.

"I determined he was more involved in atomic research than Komeil had realized, and the more I observed him, the more I realized he was a very appealing prospect for recruitment. What I wasn't able to learn, however, was the origin of his wealth. He lived in Shemiran, a luxury apartment complex north of Tehran, and drove an expensive car. He certainly didn't live the lifestyle of a scientist, but I knew if he had inherited his wealth, being approached by a wealthy businessman would probably seem very natural to him."

Carlton asked, "Was this the point at which you contacted me about Amir?"

I looked directly at Fowler.

"Yes, that's the timeline," I said. "I wanted to know if the Agency had any data on him, if NSD had any knowledge of him, if an approach on my part was warranted. It bothered me about his finances and the source of his money. I wanted our analysts to do a deep data mine on that."

"And that's when my office entered the picture," Katherine said. "I found nothing in our databases indicating his money came from any outside sources, such as Iran's intelligence agency, VEVAK, or any other ministry. We scanned everything we could find. He appeared to be clean."

Fowler stood up quickly, almost tipping over his chair.

"I need to take a break," he said in a shaky voice. "I'm sorry. I'll just be a minute."

As Fowler headed for the door, Deputy Ira gave Carlton a look I'd seen several times before—usually after receiving news a terrorist we had been tracking had just been eliminated by a drone strike.

♦ ♦ ♦ ♦

The reek of washroom soap was still clinging to Fowler's hands when he reentered the room few minutes later. Once he sat back down, he pulled a white handkerchief out of his back pocket and started cleaning his glasses.

Carlton cleared his throat and said, "Titus, resume the narrative."

Now it was about to get ugly.

The End of Chapter Five

To read the remainder of *One Night in Tehran,*
Book I in the Titus Ray Thriller Series,
order your copy from Amazon or
contact the author through email:
Author@LuanaEhrlich.com.

89096403R00105

Made in the USA
Columbia, SC
09 February 2018